Passion and Poison

Sapphire Beach Cozy Mystery Series
(Book 10)

Angela K. Ryan

John Paul Publishing

TEWKSBURY, MASSACHUSETTS

Angela K. Ryan
John Paul Publishing
Post Office Box 283
Tewksbury, MA 01876

Publisher's Note: This is a work of fiction. Names, characters, places, and incidents are a product of the author's imagination. Locales and public names are sometimes used for atmospheric purposes. Any resemblance to actual people, living or dead, or to businesses, companies, events, institutions, or locales is completely coincidental.

Passion and Poison/ Angela K. Ryan. -- 1st ed.
ISBN: 978-1-7353064-7-6

A Note of Thanks from the Author

I would like to warmly thank all those who generously shared their time and knowledge in the research of this book, especially:

Jacki Strategos, Premier Sotheby's International Realty, Marco Island

Carol Buccieri
Bella Stella Beads, Haverhill, Massachusetts

Marco Island Fire Rescue
Marco Island, Florida

Any errors are my own.

Chapter 1

ELYSE MILLER BOUNDED into *Just Jewelry* at 4:00 on a Friday afternoon in late March. Upon seeing that Connie Petretta was still in her shop, she breathed a loud sigh of relief. "I just came from a closing that took longer than I expected. Thank goodness I'm not too late."

Elyse was a realtor and had become one of Connie's best friends. Connie had relocated to Sapphire Beach in southwest Florida two years ago to open a jewelry shop, where she sold her own handmade creations, along with a growing inventory of Fair Trade product.

"Too late for what?" Abby, a part-time employee, asked.

"To see Connie before her big date with Zach tonight," Elyse said, looking at Abby as if that should have been the foremost event on everyone's mind.

Kelly, another of Connie's employees, who had been assisting a customer, joined the women, who were standing next to the circular checkout counter that sat in the center of the store. "You didn't tell us you had a special date with Zach."

"That's because I don't." Connie playfully punched Elyse in the shoulder. "Don't mind Elyse. Every single time I've had a date scheduled with Zach lately, she thinks he's going to propose."

"That's not true," Elyse said, putting her hands on her hips. A grin replaced the indignant expression she had been wearing. "Well, there might be a little truth to that. But think about it. Zach's been dropping hints about your future together for months now. And this weekend *is* the second anniversary of your first date."

"That's true," Connie said. "It's a big milestone. But think about your track record in predicting our engagement."

Elyse frowned. "I haven't been wrong *that* many times."

"Let's review," Connie said. "First, back in October when Zach's parents were visiting, you saw Zach leaving a jewelry store with a small bag and were convinced that it was an engagement ring when, in fact, it was a birthday gift for his mother."

"In all fairness, it was a logical assumption," Elyse said.

Connie held up her hand, with her palm facing Elyse. "Then you were convinced that Zach was going to propose on Christmas Eve. Then Valentine's Day."

"Yes," Elyse said. "That's all true. Maybe in the past it was wishful thinking, but this time I really feel it in my bones. You have to admit, it's a special weekend, and the two of you have a date."

"Elyse, we go out pretty much *every* weekend."

"Yes, but tonight Zach made 7:00 reservations at the *White Sands Grill.*"

"Ooh, I know that place," Kelly said. "It's an expensive gourmet restaurant with tables practically on the beach. It's nearly impossible to get reservations at 7:00, since that's shortly before the sun sets. It's going to be so romantic."

"Elyse does have a point," Abby said. "You don't go to such fancy restaurants every weekend. Your dates are usually more low-key. You'd better wear something extra special, just in case. If he does propose, you'll have those pictures forever."

Elyse took Connie's hand and examined her nails. "And maybe think about getting a manicure. You'll want to take a picture of the ring on your finger."

"I think you guys are reading too much into this," Connie said.

"Did you do anything special for your *first* anniversary?" Elyse asked.

Connie thought back. "Zach bought me roses. But I guess we didn't do anything *this* special. He was knee deep in work that week."

"I didn't tell you this before, Connie," Elyse said. "But Zach come over my house last Saturday to hang out with Josh, and he asked me a ton of questions about the resale value of his bungalow." Zach had purchased a small home situated on a canal last year. It had been in rough shape, so he got it cheap and gutted the whole thing. Connie helped him choose the finishes.

"It's perfectly logical that Zach would want to see how his investment is doing a year after he completed the renovation," Connie pointed out. "After all, he poured his entire savings, as well as his heart and soul, into renovating that house.

"Just the same," Kelly said, "I agree with Elyse. You should be ready."

Connie's mouth suddenly went dry. It was one thing to laugh off Elyse's predictions, but now both Abby and Kelly agreed with her.

"You think so?" Connie asked, suddenly taking the prospect seriously.

All three women nodded.

"Well, I guess I could leave a little early, so I have plenty of time to get ready and decide what to wear." She examined her fingernails. They were a little overdue for some attention. "I don't have time for a professional manicure, so I'll have to do it myself." Then she shook her head. "Why do I let you do this to me, Elyse? If I got a manicure every time you thought Zach was going to propose, I would be broke."

"Would it be rude if the three of us had a side bet on when Zach will propose?" Elyse asked, flashing Connie a mischievous smile.

"Um, yes," Connie said. "It would totally be rude."

Elyse chuckled. "Okay, we'll be good. Just promise you'll call me after your date if anything interesting happens." Elyse glanced at her watch. "I need to get home so I can let the sitter go."

"Give the girls a hug from me," Connie said, as Elyse was leaving.

"Will do."

Connie did her best to focus her attention on the steady stream of customers flowing in and out of the store, and not on her date later that evening. Finally, a little while after Kelly had left, there was a lull in customers, so Connie and Abby sat at the long oak table, which Connie used to create jewelry and teach her jewelry-making classes.

"Isn't Zach good friends with Elyse's husband, Josh?" Abby asked.

Connie nodded.

"Maybe she really does know something you don't know about tonight."

"Nah, Josh wouldn't tell Elyse, even if he knew Zach was up to something. He wouldn't want to put her in the position of giving her such juicy information when she couldn't tell me. Besides, if Elyse really did have that kind of news, she wouldn't be carrying on like that. She'd be avoiding me."

Abby laughed. "Well, I hope he *does* propose. I like Zach for you."

Connie felt a flash of warmth in her cheeks. So did she.

"Why don't you leave now to get ready for your date?" Abby suggested. "You know, just in case."

"I think I will. It looks like the streets are emptying out." Connie went out back to get her purse, her laptop, and Ginger's leash. Ginger was the Cavalier King Charles Spaniel, which Connie unofficially inherited from her aunt, along with her aunt's gulf-front condo. After fastening the leash on the dog, who had been chilling on her doggie bed out back, she returned to the front of the store.

As Connie was heading toward the door, she remembered that she had been meaning to ask Abby how she thought Kelly was working out.

Although Connie was pleased with her, Kelly was a new employee and she valued Abby's opinion.

Just before she reached the door, Connie turned around abruptly. "Abby."

Abby gasped and jumped back.

"Are you okay, Abby? I didn't mean to scare you." Connie studied her young employee for a moment. "I hope you don't mind my saying this, but you've been jumpy for the past week or so. Is everything okay?"

Abby let out a breath, which she had been holding. "I know. I guess it's just the stress of midterms."

"But Abby, midterms were over two weeks ago."

Abby shrugged. "Maybe it's the residual effect of all those late nights and tight deadlines."

Connie put her hand on Abby's shoulder. "I'm afraid you might be putting too much pressure on yourself. Promise me that you'll take some time to relax. You're incredibly bright, and you're going to make a fantastic professor and writer one day. Try to enjoy life in the process."

"Thanks, Connie. I promise I'll try."

Connie looked at Abby with skepticism. She wished she was more convinced that Abby would take her advice.

Beep. Beep. Beep.

This time, both Connie and Abby were startled.

"What on earth is that?" Abby asked.

Connie peered out through the display window and glanced up and down the street. "I have no idea, but it's definitely coming from outside."

"Maybe it's a car alarm," Abby said, as she followed Connie to the door.

Connie pointed across the street. "No, it's coming from *Gallagher's*."

They both watched as a stream of Gallagher's customers filed down the wooden staircase leading from *Gallagher's Tropical Shack* to the sidewalk.

"Oh, no! Poor Gallagher. It's dinnertime on a Friday during one of our busiest months of the year, and his smoke detector is chasing patrons from his restaurant. That can't be good for business."

Connie stepped outside and watched as a few people headed in the direction of the parking lot down the street. "I hope those people paid their tab and aren't taking advantage of a fire alarm to skip out on paying."

"I guess there's nothing Gallagher can do about that," Abby said. "He's going to have his hands full trying to reassure his remaining customers."

"Hopefully, it was just caused by too much smoke in the kitchen and he can reopen right away. I know Gallagher hired a new head cook a few months ago," Connie said.

Gallagher exited his restaurant after the last customer. "I'm sorry that your meal was interrupted, folks. I'm sure this will be resolved in no time. To make up for it, I'll give you a free drink or dessert on the house."

A mini-cheer erupted from the small crowd. Most people seemed to be handling the situation in stride. That is, everyone except one man who was complaining rather loudly. "This is ridiculous," he said, getting into Gallagher's space. "So much for a relaxing meal."

"I'm sorry, sir, but better safe than sorry."

Another man put his hand on the first man's shoulder. "Come on, Arnold. It's not his fault."

Connie didn't envy Gallagher's predicament.

Within a couple of minutes, sirens sounded in the distance, followed soon after by a Sapphire Beach Fire Rescue truck, which parked in front of *Gallagher's Tropical Shack*.

Two uniformed men rushed in, and within a few minutes, the smoke detector was silenced.

"It's okay, folks," one of the first responders said. "It was just a false alarm. It's all clear to go back inside."

Gallagher shook the men's hands and Connie could hear him thanking them for resolving the situation so quickly. Then Gallagher stood at the entrance and ushered the customers back inside.

Before long, it appeared that things were back to normal.

Gallagher glanced over and noticed Connie standing there watching, so she gave him a reassuring wave.

He pretended to wipe the sweat from his forehead in an exaggerated motion and Connie laughed. She was glad to see that he was taking the potential fiasco with good humor.

Abby had been assisting customers while Connie was watching the drama unfold across the street, so she went back inside to update Abby.

"Everything seems to be okay," Connie said to Abby and the customers. "Something in the kitchen must have set off the smoke detector, but everyone's going back inside."

"I'm glad to hear it," Abby said, walking a woman to the checkout counter and ringing up her purchase. "Poor Gallagher. A Friday afternoon in March is not a good time to have lost business."

Connie nodded her agreement.

"Now go get ready for your big date with Zach," Abby said. "I've got things under control here."

"Ooh, a big date," the customer said, slipping her purchase into her purse. "It's been ages since I've had a big date. Have fun."

Connie grinned at the woman. "Thank you."

As Connie and Ginger began walking down the sidewalk toward Connie's car, she was startled by the sound of a shrill scream coming from inside Gallagher's restaurant. She quickly switched directions and picked up her pace. As she passed by *Just Jewelry*, Connie opened the door to let Ginger inside, shrugged at Abby, and jogged across the street to *Gallagher's*.

She mounted the stairs, two steps at a time, and stopped at the hostess desk, where she had a full view of the restaurant. Everybody's eyes were fixed on a table at the back of the dining room.

At first, Connie couldn't see what the problem was. Until she looked down at the floor and noticed a man lying motionless on his side.

It was Arnold, the same man who was giving Gallagher a hard time earlier about his meal being interrupted because of the alarm.

Gallagher was kneeling next to Arnold with his hand on the man's neck.

"I can't find a pulse," he yelled. "Hurry! Somebody, call 9-1-1."

Chapter 2

THE THREE MEN who were seated at the table remained as still as Arnold, who hadn't moved a muscle since Connie had set eyes on him.

Seeing that nobody was budging, Connie yanked her phone from her purse and dialed 9-1-1. Once she was assured that help was on its way, she stepped back to survey the scene.

A murmur made its way through the crowd.

"Do you think he's dead?" one woman asked.

"He looks familiar," another patron commented. "Where have I seen him before?"

"Is there a doctor in the house?" Gallagher finally managed, in a commanding voice.

The room fell silent.

One of the men seated at Arnold's table lowered himself to the floor. "Hang in there, buddy. Help is on the way."

Connie glanced back into the kitchen. The two cooks, whom she had seen earlier during the fire drill, were now standing next to the bar staring at the victim, entranced. The servers, the hostess, and all the customers also looked as if they were in freeze frame. It felt like time had stopped inside *Gallagher's Tropical Shack*.

The sound of sirens pierced the silence, and for the second time in less than a half hour, a white and red truck with "Sapphire Beach Fire Rescue" printed on the side parked in front of Gallagher's restaurant.

When they saw Arnold on the floor, they rushed over.

"He seemed to have some kind of a seizure, then he collapsed and fell to the ground," one of Arnold's dinner companions said.

The paramedics checked for a pulse but apparently couldn't find one. One of them attempted to revive the man with CPR, while the other brought in a defibrillator, but their efforts were in vain.

"I'm sorry," one of the first responders said to the three men who had apparently been dining with Arnold. "He's dead."

A woman seated at the next table watched the scene unfold with tears in her eyes. Connie wondered if she knew the deceased man, or if her tears were simply a result of watching a man die. The woman fixed her gaze on Arnold's friends, who were still staring at their dinner companion with their jaws hanging open.

Just then, a patrol officer arrived on the scene and made quick work of ushering everyone onto the sidewalk and stringing yellow tape across the entrance to the restaurant. The police officer ordered Gallagher's patrons not to leave and within a few minutes, Zach arrived on the scene, followed soon after by Josh and Sergeant Tim Donahue.

Connie had completely forgotten that she had been on her way home to get ready for her date with Zach until she saw him get out of his car.

There was no chance they would make their 7:00 dinner reservations now.

Next, the medical examiner arrived.

Zach instructed them to make a pathway from the street to the restaurant so the medical examiner, and later the crime scene technicians, could get through.

While Connie waited to give her statement, she checked her phone and noticed a few texts from Abby, who wanted to know why Fire Rescue had shown up at *Gallagher's* for a second time in one evening.

Connie explained as best she could in a text but promised to come over with more information as soon as she was able.

There was a lot of chatter among the crowd, but nobody seemed to know anything that shed light on what happened. From the information Connie gleaned by talking with some of the people present, nobody noticed anything unusual until Arnold began convulsing and fell to the ground, which happened shortly after he began eating his salad. The consensus among bystanders seemed to be that Arnold's salad was poisoned.

"The killer must have done it during the fire alarm," one man said. "It was probably a decoy to give him access to the man's salad."

However, there was one thing that everyone agreed on. The victim was Arnold Burton, a famous tennis pro who had been popular about fifteen years ago.

After nearly an hour of talking with those who were in closest proximity to the victim at the time of his death, including Gallagher, Zach walked over to where Connie was standing. He escorted her further down the sidewalk, where they could talk privately.

"How are you holding up?" he asked. "Gallagher said you came in as everything was going down."

"I was on my way to my car when I heard the commotion, so I came over to see what was happening. I'm worried about Gallagher." She glanced over at her friend, who was normally a healthy ball of energy. He looked pale and somehow smaller.

"I am, too," Zach said. "Unfortunately, we're going to have to close down his restaurant for the time being. He's going to need a friend."

"I'll invite him and Stephanie to my place tonight so we can help him decompress," Connie said.

"That's a good idea. I'm obviously going to be tied up here for the rest of the night. I'm so sorry we have to postpone our date. I had a special evening planned for our second anniversary."

"I'll call the restaurant and cancel our reservation," Connie said.

"Thanks. How about if we do it next weekend instead?"

"I'd like that."

Some of the disappointment receded from Zach's eyes as they made plans for the following weekend. He started to walk away, then turned abruptly. "I almost forgot. I also came over to ask what you saw tonight."

Connie recounted everything she saw and heard, beginning with the fire.

"Does the medical examiner think Arnold was murdered?" Connie asked, when she finished giving her statement.

Zach nodded. "Judging from the manner in which he died, and since, according to his friends, he was in perfect health, it's likely that he was poisoned. They said he seemed healthy and energetic right up until he started eating his food. Then the situation deteriorated quickly. The medical examiner thinks his salad might have been laced with something deadly, so we are sending it to be analyzed. They'll be performing an autopsy as soon as possible, as well."

"How long will Gallagher's restaurant be closed?"

"It's hard to say. Right now, it's a crime scene. What happens after that will depend upon what we and the Board of Health discover."

"Gallagher's not a suspect, is he?" Connie asked.

"No. He was never alone with Arnold's food."

"Do you think someone poisoned the food during the chaos of the fire alarm?"

"We don't know yet, but it's obviously a strong possibility. According to witnesses, Arnold's salad was already in front of him when the alarm went off, and it was just sitting at the table while everyone vacated the restaurant. Since it was a cold meal, Arnold didn't bother to send it back to be reheated, as some of the other patrons did."

Connie glanced back over at Gallagher, who looked like he was barely holding it together.

"Can I talk to Gallagher before I leave?"

"Of course."

When she and Zach finished talking, Connie walked up behind Gallagher and put her arm around his shoulder. “How are you doing, my friend?”

“This is a nightmare, Connie. It was awful. I don’t know what happened to Arnold, but that is not a pleasant way to go. How could I have let this happen in my restaurant?”

“It wasn’t your fault, Gallagher.”

“Maybe not, but all the bad publicity the restaurant is sure to acquire could put me out of business. Even if it doesn’t, we’re in the middle of the tourist season. I certainly can’t afford to be closed down until a murder case is solved.”

Connie squeezed his shoulder. “Hang in there. I know it’s easier said than done, but try not to imagine the worst.”

“I’ll do my best.”

“It sounds like the police will be letting everyone leave soon. I’m heading back to my place. How about if I call Stephanie and Grace, and we meet you at my condo after you finish here? We can talk this through.”

Gallagher forced a smile. “Thank you. I could use some friendly support right now.”

She gave him a warm hug. “Come over as soon as you can. We’ll be there.”

Connie went back to *Just Jewelry* to get Ginger and to fill Abby in on what had taken place.

“I was watching from the window in between customers,” Abby said. “When I saw Zach arrive, I figured that your date was off.”

“It’s just as well. I couldn’t celebrate my anniversary with Zach knowing what Gallagher was going through.”

“Stephanie and Grace are going to be crushed, too,” Abby said.

“This couldn’t have happened at a worse time. After years of living modestly and investing every penny he earned back into the restaurant, he bought a condo just before Christmas and was finally taking time off to enjoy life and spend time with Stephanie.”

“Maybe the police will get to the bottom of what happened quickly, and he’ll be able to reopen in a few days,” Abby said.

“Let’s hope so,” Connie said, attaching Ginger’s leash. But judging from her previous experiences with murder cases, they were rarely solved in a few days. “Ginger and I had better go. Gallagher’s coming over to my house tonight, and I want to make sure Stephanie and Grace are there when he arrives.”

An hour later, Gallagher, Stephanie, and Grace were gathered in Connie’s living room, and Gallagher was catching Stephanie and Grace up on his traumatic evening.

“They didn’t say for sure,” Gallagher said, “but it sounded to me like the police are thinking that Arnold was murdered.”

“You’re right,” Connie said. “After I gave my statement, I asked Zach what the medical examiner said, and that’s the direction they seem to be leaning.”

“That’s the Connie I know and love,” Stephanie said. “See, Gallagher? She’s already on top of this investigation.”

“Of course,” Connie said. “You don’t think I would leave Gallagher high and dry? Besides, I was thinking about it as I walked Ginger. There can’t be many people who were both at the restaurant tonight *and* had a motive to kill Arnold Burton. Maybe this case won’t be that difficult to solve.”

"Nobody who works in my restaurant would have a motive to kill Arnold," Gallagher said. "It would have to be someone who was dining with him."

"Let's go over that," Connie said. "If Arnold's salad was poisoned, who would have had access to his food?"

"There were two cooks in the kitchen," Gallagher said. "Fernando, the head cook, and Manny. I suppose they both could have had the opportunity to poison the salad, but why would they do that? I heard them talking to the police. They both said that they had never even met Arnold before."

"That's probably true," Connie said. "But for now, let's not worry about motive. Let's determine who had access to the food."

"What about the server?" Stephanie asked. "She could have slipped something in the food while she brought Arnold his order."

Gallagher shook his head. "That's impossible. Penelope didn't bring them their food. The food runner did, and I had eyes on him the whole time he carried their plates. I had hopped onto the floor to help out, because we got a rush of customers. I was delivering appetizers to a table next to Arnold's, and

I saw the food runner deliver the salad to Arnold. He was never alone with the food, and he was carrying several other plates at the same time. There's no way he could have done it."

"Okay, well that's something," Connie said. "Out of all your employees, the only ones who could possibly have done it are your cooks. It's unlikely that they had a motive, but we can't completely rule them out until we know for sure. Now, what about the three men who were with Arnold? I heard some customers say that Arnold's food had already been delivered when the fire alarm went off."

"That's right," Gallagher said.

"So, any of them could have profited from the chaos of the alarm to poison the salad," Stephanie added.

Gallagher nodded. "That's true. And there was also a woman seated at the next table who came over to greet Arnold and his friends just before their food was delivered. They definitely knew each other. She was still at the table when the alarm went off, and she was sitting right next to Arnold."

"Maybe there were two killers," Grace suggested. "One who pulled the alarm and another who poisoned the salad."

"That's possible," Gallagher said. "I asked the first responders what they thought set off the alarm, and they said it was likely caused by too much smoke coming from the kitchen. But I'm telling you, there wasn't any smoke."

"Then the alarm definitely could have been a decoy," Stephanie said.

"I was sitting within earshot when Zach questioned Arnold's friends," Gallagher said. "Apparently, two of them were partners with Arnold in a tennis magazine and the fourth man is a writer for the publication. Ronnie and Dom were the co-owners with Arnold, and Evan is a staff writer. Evan had stepped outside to make a phone call just before the food was delivered. He was still outside when the alarm went off, so he has an alibi."

"That leaves Ronnie, Dom, and the woman from the next table," Connie said. "I remember her. I was watching her as Arnold was lying on the ground. She was visibly upset."

Stephanie narrowed her eyes. “Arnold, Ronnie, Dom, and Evan. Those names sound familiar.”

“Apparently, they come to Sapphire Beach every year on some sort of working vacation,” Gallagher said. “I heard they’re renting a bungalow on a canal.”

Stephanie’s eyes flew open. “That’s why their names sound familiar. Their vacation rental is on my street. They’ve come for two weeks every March for as long as I’ve lived there.”

“Do you know them?” Connie asked.

“We’ve chatted a few times. Those guys are a lot of fun. They know many of the tennis pros in town because of their magazine, so they have access to any court they want in Sapphire Beach. They come to town to play tennis and to catch some matches. I once heard them bragging that they write off the entire trip, even though they don’t work a whole lot. From what I hear, Arnold was really successful on the tournament circuit back in the day.”

“Do you think you could get them to talk to us?” Connie asked.

“It’s worth a shot. I’ll do my best.”

"This is probably going to sound selfish, but I really hope it was one of them and not one of my cooks," Gallagher said.

"Chances are it was," Connie said. "What motive could your cooks possibly have?"

Gallagher stared silently into the darkness through Connie's living room sliders.

"Gallagher, is there something you're not telling us?" Connie asked.

He stood up, put his hands in the pocket of his grey pants and stood by the window. "I feel guilty even thinking this, but my head cook, Fernando, has a police record. When he came for the job interview, he seemed like he was trying to get his life back in order, so I gave him a chance. I hope that wasn't a big mistake."

"We'll talk to Fernando, too," Connie said. "Don't worry. We're going to get to the bottom of this."

Chapter 3

AFTER EVERYONE HAD LEFT Connie's condo, she was getting ready for bed when her phone rang in the other room. She threw on her pajamas and dashed over to the coffee table, where she had left her cell phone.

Elyse's name appeared on the screen.

With everything that took place that evening, Connie completely forgot to tell Elyse that her date with Zach never happened. She tapped on the green "answer" icon and cut Elyse off before she could ask about her date. "Before you ask me if I got engaged tonight..."

Elyse interrupted her. "I know. Josh just got home. No proposal."

Connie had to laugh at the fact that Elyse seemed more disappointed than Connie was. “Try to keep things in perspective, Elyse. A guy just died.”

“Oh, I know. What happened to Arnold Burton is awful. I was just hoping we’d be talking about wedding plans tonight and not a murder investigation. Please at least tell me that you and Zach rescheduled the date.”

Connie plopped down onto an armchair and patted her lap so Ginger would hop up. “We postponed it until next Friday. I’m not worried about Zach and me. We’ll still have our anniversary date. But I *am* worried about Gallagher. This could be disastrous to his business, just as everything was finally going his way. He just bought a home, he and Stephanie recently found each other, and now this.”

“Josh said that the Board of Health would likely close down the restaurant until they could be certain that what happened wasn’t Gallagher’s fault.”

“That’s what Zach said, too. And since it’s the height of tourist and snowbird season in Florida right now, he stands to lose a lot of money.”

"I imagine you're planning to investigate," Elyse said.

"Do you even have to ask?" Connie filled Elyse in on what she knew so far and their plans to talk to Arnold's friends, as well as Gallagher's head cook, Fernando.

"It doesn't sound like there's a huge pool of suspects," Elyse said. "It had to be one of Arnold's friends or the woman who came over to say hello. It seems unlikely that anyone else in the restaurant would have had a motive."

"I guess we'll find that out soon enough. The victim was staying at a rented bungalow on Stephanie's street with some friends. We're going to try to talk to them ASAP. They would know if Arnold had any enemies who were present at *Gallagher's* tonight. I'm hoping we can talk with Evan first. He was outside taking a phone call when Arnold's salad was delivered, so he never had access to it. He's the most likely to tell us the truth."

"Keep me posted on the investigation and I'll keep my ears open with Josh, although he never tells me anything about his cases."

"I will."

"But more importantly, keep me posted on any news with Zach. I can't believe I have to wait another whole week to see if he's going to propose."

Connie shook her head and laughed. "Good night, Elyse."

The following morning while Connie was eating breakfast, her phone pinged with a text message. It was a group text from Stephanie to Connie and Gallagher.

I just saw Evan head to the beach for his morning walk. If you guys can come over right now, we could probably catch him alone on his way back.

Connie glanced at the time on the microwave. She still had more than an hour before she had to be at work.

Within fifteen minutes, both Connie and Gallagher were sitting with Stephanie on her front porch.

"Evan has to pass this way to get back to his vacation rental," Stephanie said. "I'll get us some lemonade in case it takes a while. Yell inside the house if you see him coming before I get back."

When Stephanie returned carrying a tray holding three glasses filled with ice and a pitcher of pink lemonade, Connie stood and held the door for her. As she started to close the door, she noticed a tennis racket inside the entryway next to the front door. She picked it up and brought it outside.

"I forgot you play tennis," Connie said, twisting the racket in her hand. "You'll have to teach me sometime."

"Anytime," Stephanie said.

After a half hour, Evan emerged in the distance.

"There he is!" Stephanie cried.

As Evan drew closer to the house, Connie walked to the end of Stephanie's walkway and stood on the sidewalk, where Evan couldn't miss her. Stephanie and Gallagher followed suit.

"Hi Evan," Connie said with the tennis racket still in hand.

Evan stared at her for a moment, as if he were trying to place her. Then he glanced at Gallagher, and recognition dawned on his face.

"Gallagher, I didn't expect to see you here," Evan said.

"Stephanie is my girlfriend. My friend, Connie, and I were just visiting when we saw you walk by. I wanted to extend my condolences once again. I promise you that my restaurant follows the strictest safety guidelines. I am committed to finding out what happened to Arnold."

Evan smiled politely. "Thank you," he said, and started to leave.

Connie stepped forward. "Would we be able to talk to you for a few minutes?"

Evan glanced towards his rental house and then back at Connie. "I suppose," he hesitated. While they were walking to Stephanie's front porch, he pointed to the racket in Connie's hand. "Do you play?"

Connie shook her head and chuckled. "This is Stephanie's tennis racket. I've never played in my life. But hopefully someday I'll have the time to learn."

Evan held out his hand, gesturing for her to give him the racket, and Connie handed it to him.

"Here, you can start practicing even before you step foot on the court. Let me show you a single-handed backhand." He stood next to Connie. "It looks like you're right-handed."

Connie nodded.

"In that case, when you see the ball coming to your left side, you turn like this," Evan said, turning his right shoulder, "and move toward the ball sideways. Then, be sure your racket head is above the grip, so you have leverage over the ball. Support the racket with your left hand, like this." He put his left hand on the throat of the racket. "Then swing. Make sure your left hand goes backwards for counterbalance, but keep your body sideways, like this," he said, demonstrating in slow motion.

Evan handed Connie the racket. "You try."

After she gave it a try and Evan gave her a few more pointers, he followed them to Stephanie's front porch.

"I'm sure you didn't call me over to ask for tennis pointers," Evan said. "I'm guessing you wanted to talk about last night."

"We were hoping that since you were friends with Arnold, that you might have some idea of what happened," Gallagher said.

Evan took a deep breath and ran his hand through his sandy blond hair.

"I know this must be a difficult time for you," Stephanie said. "I was so sorry to hear about Arnold.

I always enjoyed when the four of you came to Sapphire Beach. You liven up the neighborhood in the best of ways."

"We love coming here. When we told them about Arnold, our loved ones back home in California tried to get us to leave early. We rented the house for two weeks, and we've only been here for one so far. But we decided to stay through the second week. We thought we could better honor Arnold's life if we were together, and the medical examiner hasn't released the body yet, so the funeral services have been delayed, anyway."

"Was Arnold married?" Stephanie asked.

Evan smirked. "Arnold was more of a free spirit. He never wanted to be tied down."

"We understand you all work together at a tennis magazine," Connie said.

"That's right. The magazine is called *Tennis Times.* Ronnie and Dom put up the capital for the magazine, and Arnold was the big draw. When they founded the magazine fifteen years ago, Arnold was still a big deal in the tennis world."

"So, you're not an owner?" Connie asked.

Evan laughed. "I wish. No, I'm just a poor writer. Unless I'm traveling for work, I can't afford a vacation like this. Ronnie, Dom, and Arnold were the owners. Now it's just Ronnie and Dom." Evan studied Connie for a moment. "You look familiar. Didn't I see you at *Gallagher's* last night?"

"Yes. I own the jewelry shop across the street. When that woman shrieked, I came over to see what was going on. Then I had to stay put until I could give the police my statement." Connie looked directly at Evan. "I hope you know that Gallagher is devastated that this happened in his restaurant. We've figured out who had access to Arnold's food last night, but not having known Arnold, we don't know who might have wanted to hurt him."

"Of course, we know that you couldn't have done it," Gallagher said.

"Ah, I see," Evan said. "That's why you wanted to talk to me first."

"We were hoping you could tell us if Arnold had any enemies who were present last night," Connie said.

Evan let out a deep sigh. "I've been asking myself the same question ever since it happened. Arnold didn't show any signs, whatsoever, of being sick until after he started eating his salad. As you said, the killer would have to have both been at the restaurant last night *and* had a motive to kill him."

"Is there anyone you can think of who fits both of those categories?" Gallagher asked.

Evan stared at the ground. "I think I'm afraid to think about it too much, because there aren't many people who fit both of those categories. And three of them are my friends."

"*Three* of them?" Connie asked.

Evan nodded.

"I assume you are referring to Dom and Ronnie," Connie said. "Do you also mean the woman who came over from the next table to say hello while you stepped outside for your phone call?"

"Yes. That was Kendra. She's also a tennis pro."

"Let's start with Ronnie and Dom," Connie said. "Did either of them have a motive to kill Arnold?"

Evan leaned back in his chair and let out a long breath. "They both had a reason to want Arnold out of the picture. But if you ask me, Dom's motive was more compelling."

Chapter 4

CONNIE, GALLAGHER, AND STEPHANIE looked expectantly at Evan, who was gazing toward a Bismarck palm tree in Stephanie's front yard.

Evan returned his attention to his hosts. "Let me give you some background. As I mentioned, Arnold was a free spirit. He didn't exactly pull his weight with the magazine. Ronnie and Dom provided the capital, but they brought Arnold on board for his name and reputation. It was a smart business move, and we gained much of our readership because of Arnold's involvement. He was a great PR man and well-loved within the tennis community. He also loved traveling to promote the magazine. It was the perfect job for Arnold - tennis trips on the company credit card, increased popularity - he loved the lifestyle."

"I don't understand," Gallagher said. "Won't the magazine lose readers now that Arnold is gone? It sounds like Arnold was more useful to Ronnie and Dom alive."

"That's just it. They don't need him anymore. Over the years, *Tennis Times* has grown into a well-respected magazine. Even without Arnold, it will probably remain strong."

"But still," Connie persisted, "wouldn't it have been stronger with Arnold around to promote it?"

"It might have," Evan said, "if Dom and Ronnie didn't want to sell the magazine. The three owners recently received a generous offer to purchase it. Ronnie and Dom wanted to accept it, especially Dom. Ronnie is eager to retire early, but Dom's financial needs are, let's just say, more urgent."

"What do you mean?" Connie asked.

"Dom is in over his head with gambling debt."

"Let me guess," Gallagher said. "Arnold refused to sell."

"That's right. Arnold wasn't ready to give up the celebrity lifestyle, and he also didn't think much of the person who wanted to purchase it. But she's very persistent," Evan said. She even followed us here this week to try to convince Arnold to change his mind. If you haven't guessed by now, Kendra is the potential buyer."

"The woman seated at the next table?" Gallagher asked.

"That's the one. But as persistent as Kendra can be, Arnold wasn't budging."

"How persistent was she?" Connie asked.

Evan smirked and shook his head. "It's no secret that we come here every year, so she worked her vacation around our schedule. She followed us here to Sapphire Beach. Over the past week, she..." Evan made air quotes with his fingers. "Coincidently showed up at many of the same events we've gone to. I wasn't surprised to see her at *Gallagher's* last night."

"So, Kendra has a motive, too," Connie said.

Evan nodded. "She wants the magazine something fierce. Ronnie and Dom had been stalling her, because they were trying to convince Arnold to sell. They hoped that once they got to Sapphire Beach, Arnold would relax and reconsider Kendra's offer. But it quickly became evident that Arnold wasn't going to budge."

"Do you think she wanted the magazine enough to kill for it?" Gallagher asked.

Evan shrugged his shoulders. "I can't say for sure. But she wanted it enough to follow us to Sapphire Beach."

"Evan, I hope you don't mind my asking you this," Connie said. "But last night during the fire alarm, Arnold made quite a scene on the sidewalk over the inconvenience of having to evacuate the building."

"I remember."

"I don't want to speak ill of the dead, but was he always that challenging?"

"Those little tantrums were normal for Arnold. He didn't like it when things didn't go his way. Let's just say, those who were close to him had to accept that about him." Evan glanced at his watch. "If that's all, I'd better get going, or Ronnie and Dom will wonder what's taking me so long."

"Just one more question before you leave," Connie said. "Besides the three of you and Kendra, did Arnold know anyone else who was in the restaurant last night?"

"Only Fernando," Evan said. "But he didn't know him very well."

Gallagher looked as though someone had punched him in the stomach. "*Fernando*? You mean my head cook?"

"Yes. When we saw him, we thought about leaving due to Arnold's and Fernando's history. But Arnold insisted it would be fine."

"What do you mean?" Connie asked. "What history?"

"During a trip to Sapphire Beach four or five years ago, we went to *Seaview Restaurant*. Arnold ordered salmon and said it was overcooked, so he sent it back and demanded that the chef make it again. As I said, Arnold was known for these little temper tantrums. He was way out of line. I mean, it *was* an expensive meal, so I don't blame him for sending it back. It was just the way he did it. Anyway, apparently, it wasn't the first time someone sent back a meal that Fernando had cooked. I guess it was the straw that broke the camel's back, because the restaurant manager fired Fernando on the spot. I felt bad for the guy. We never saw him again until last night."

Gallagher leaned back in his chair, speechless.

Both Connie and Stephanie kept quiet about Fernando having a police record.

"I didn't even know Fernando worked at *Seaview*," Gallagher said. "It wasn't listed on his application."

"Nobody lists a place of employment that they got fired from on a job application," Stephanie said.

"Good point."

"We won't take up any more of your time, Evan," Connie said. "Thank you for talking with us. Would it be okay if we contacted you if any other questions come up?"

"Sure," Evan said. "Despite his quirks, Arnold was really good to me over the years. In fact, he was the one who convinced Ronnie and Dom to give me a chance when I was a brand-new writer. As I told the police, I'll do whatever I can to help."

Evan gave Connie his phone number, and she entered it in her phone.

"Be careful, Evan," Stephanie said, as he was leaving. "You could be staying with a killer."

Evan turned around and smiled. "I appreciate your concern, but I doubt either of them would hurt me. If something happened to me, it would make it obvious that one of them was the killer. But I will stay vigilant."

After Evan left, Connie and Gallagher helped Stephanie bring the lemonade glasses from earlier back into the house, and Connie put Stephanie's tennis racket back in the entryway, where she had found it.

"What do you think?" Stephanie asked, while she loaded the glasses into the dishwasher and rinsed out the pitcher.

"We have four viable suspects, but for the sake of Gallagher's restaurant, I hope Fernando didn't do it," Connie said.

"How well do you know Fernando?" Stephanie asked Gallagher.

He leaned against the wall. "I guess not that well. I only hired him a few months ago. We talk a lot while we're cleaning up at the end of the night. He's a hard worker, and he's really trying to get his life back on track after his incarceration. He hopes to open his own restaurant at some point down the line, so he's always asking questions about the business side of things. I hope he didn't just blow his future over petty revenge."

"Cheer up, Gallagher," Connie said. "There's a good chance Fernando isn't guilty. At this point, Dom seems to have the strongest motive out of all four of them."

"And don't forget about Ronnie and Kendra," Stephanie said. "Their motives aren't as strong as Dom's, but they still had their reasons for wanting Arnold out of the picture."

"That's right," Connie said. "Kendra knew that Arnold was the reason the men weren't accepting her offer to purchase *Tennis Times*, so she could have decided to take matters into her own hands."

"Or maybe Ronnie realized that as long as Arnold was in the picture, he'd never be able to retire early," Stephanie added. "Every one of them had access to Arnold's food and a motive."

"I guess that makes me feel a little better," Gallagher said. "But for my own peace of mind, I'd like to talk to Fernando and my other cook, Manny, before we attempt to talk with Dom and Ronnie. Hopefully, we can rule Fernando out early on."

"Why don't we start with Manny?" Connie suggested. "He didn't have a motive to kill Arnold, so he's more likely to be truthful with us. He might have seen something, since he was working in the kitchen with Fernando."

"Okay," Gallagher agreed. "But we'll have to tread delicately. As much as I hate to say it, Manny and Fernando have become good friends since I hired Fernando, so even if he did see something suspicious, Manny might not have told the police. I think he'd be more likely to confide in me."

Connie glanced at the clock on Stephanie's stove. "Yikes, it's already 9:00! I'd better text Grace to let her know I'm running late. If you guys want to go to Manny's now, I can let her know that I'll be a little while longer."

"That would be amazing," Gallagher said. "I know where he lives. I'll drive."

Chapter 5

CONNIE, STEPHANIE, AND GALLAGHER made the half hour drive to Fort Myers, where Manny lived. Gallagher's GPS brought them to an older, low rise apartment building with a catwalk that stretched around its perimeter.

"This is it," Gallagher said, pulling into a parking spot marked *visitor*. "Manny lives in unit 217."

They climbed the outdoor staircase and followed the catwalk around until they found Manny's apartment.

Gallagher knocked on the door.

"Yeah, who is it?" came a voice from inside.

"Manny, it's Gallagher. Could I talk to you for a few minutes?"

"Sure thing, boss."

The deadbolt clicked, and a short, stout man with dark hair and a mustache, who Connie guessed was in his mid-thirties, opened the door.

Manny gestured for them to follow him inside the tiny apartment. "I would have straightened up if I knew you were coming, boss. Although, I can't say I'm surprised. I figured you'd want to talk about what happened last night."

"You know Stephanie," Gallagher said. "This is our friend, Connie."

Connie extended her hand. "Hi, Manny. It's nice to meet you. I'm sorry it's under these circumstances."

"Me, too," Manny said. "I still can't believe a guy just keeled over and died right during dinner. Do you have any idea when we will be able to reopen?"

Gallagher shook his head apologetically. "We're closed until further notice. Right now, the restaurant is a crime scene, and after the police release it, we'll be investigated by the Board of Health. That's why we came by. Connie has a pretty good track record for solving murders in Sapphire Beach, and I've asked her to help me look into things."

A *flawless* track record, actually. But it wasn't the time to argue semantics.

Manny's eyes flew open. "Oh, *she's* the one you're always talking about. It was good thinking to call her in."

Gallagher smiled and playfully elbowed Connie. "See how I brag about my friends?"

"I hope you can solve this one fast and get us all back to work," Manny said. "Some of the staff and I were talking last night while we waited to give our statements, and none of us can afford to be without a paycheck for very long."

"We'll do our best," Connie said. "For now, we're casting the net wide and trying to talk to anyone who could have witnessed anything unusual. Since you were in the kitchen, Manny, we wondered if you saw anything suspicious last night."

"You mean besides the guy croaking in the restaurant?"

Connie bit her cheek to keep herself from laughing. "Yes, besides that."

"Well, I didn't see who set off that phony smoke detector, but if you ask me, it's probably the same person who killed that guy," Manny said.

"What do you mean by *phony* alarm?" Connie asked.

"The Fire Rescue folks said that it was likely caused from smoke coming from the kitchen, but there was no smoke anywhere when that thing went off. Somebody had to have pulled the lever."

"And you think that whoever set it off probably did it as a decoy?" Connie asked.

"Bingo," Manny said.

"Where are the levers located?" Connie asked Gallagher.

"Besides the one in my office, there's one outside the kitchen and another outside the restrooms, on the opposite side of the restaurant," he replied. Then Gallagher addressed Manny. "I know you've become friends with Fernando since you began working together, and that you think highly of him. But I have a question that I need you to answer truthfully. Did Fernando tell you that he knew Arnold Burton, the man who was killed?"

Manny turned his head away from Gallagher and stared at the floor.

"You can trust us, Manny," Gallagher said.

Manny ran both hands through his thin dark hair. "Oh, I really hope Fernando didn't do anything stupid. Yeah, he told me he knew the dude as soon as he walked into the restaurant. Fernando said that the dead guy got him fired from his job a while back. He had trouble finding a job after that, and that's when he got busted robbing that convenient store."

"Manny, are you saying that Fernando getting fired because of Arnold led to him committing the burglary that landed him in jail?" Gallagher asked.

"Yup. Fernando told me the robbery was four years ago. You do the math. I figured it all out while I was waiting to talk to the police. But if you ask me, Fernando wouldn't have killed a guy over that. He was trying to get his life back together and was grateful that you gave him the job. A lot of people wouldn't hire him after he got out of prison."

"I hope it wasn't a mistake," Gallagher said.

Stephanie put her hand on Gallagher's shoulder.

"Would Fernando have had any way of knowing which food order was Arnold's?" Connie asked.

"The orders are printed in the kitchen with table numbers on them, so he would at least know the table," Gallagher said.

"He definitely knew which meal was Arnold's," Manny said. "Fernando insisted on making it himself, and then, after the alarm, I saw him watching the guy eat the salad. I remember because I looked up and didn't see Fernando anywhere, so I went looking for him. He had stepped just outside the kitchen and was staring at Arnold while he ate."

"This doesn't sound good," Gallagher said.

"Manny, this is important. Were you watching Fernando while he made Arnold's salad?" Connie asked.

"I mean, the kitchen's not that big, and we were facing each other while we worked. But I can't say I was watching every single second. Plus, I was talking to that woman for a minute who wandered into the kitchen."

"What woman?" Gallagher asked. "Patrons aren't allowed in the kitchen."

"I know," Manny said. "That's what I told her. She said she was looking for the ladies' room."

"But the restrooms are on the other side of the restaurant," Connie said.

Manny shrugged. "I guess she was lost. It's not the first time that's happened. People are dumber than they look, you know. They don't pay attention when you're giving them directions. Fernando offered to show her the way. He said he had to go, anyway."

"So, Fernando left the kitchen for a few minutes just before the fire alarm went off?" Connie asked.

"Yup. But he was only gone for a few minutes. He was back in the kitchen by the time it went off."

"What did the woman look like?" Connie asked.

"She was a real looker. She had long, dark brown hair and blue eyes." Manny chuckled. "I think that's why Fernando personally escorted her to the ladies' room. I'll bet he tried to get her number."

"I don't remember seeing a woman matching that description while we were waiting on the sidewalk," Connie said.

"Me, either," Gallagher said.

"That's because she wasn't there. Fernando looked for her after the fire alarm, but I don't think she ever came back. I wonder if she's the one who pulled the alarm."

"The lever for the alarm is right outside the restrooms, so it's possible," Gallagher said. "And Arnold's table was at the back of the dining room, near the restroom, so she would have had to have walked right past it to exit the building."

"That means that, theoretically, this woman could have come in off the street and pulled the alarm to create a decoy, then poisoned Arnold's food on the way out," Connie said.

"But why would she go into the kitchen first? If she was the killer, she would have wanted to avoid being seen," Stephanie said.

"Maybe she really did end up in the kitchen by accident," Gallagher suggested.

"For that matter, I suppose anyone could have pulled the alarm to cause a distraction and poisoned Arnold's food on their way out," Connie pointed out. "I saw several people leaving in the middle of the alarm. Any one of them could have been the killer."

Gallagher folded his arms. "If that's true, that means that the killer wouldn't necessarily have been in the restaurant after the alarm. It could be someone we haven't even considered yet."

"We really need to find that woman," Connie said. "If she's the one who set off the alarm, then we'll know that this mystery woman is either the killer, or that the killer had to be in the restaurant after the alarm."

"But if she didn't pull the alarm, then it's possible the killer pulled it, poisoned Arnold's food on the way out, then left the restaurant during all the confusion," Gallagher said. "Otherwise, the only people with access to Arnold's food were the cooks and those sitting at Arnold's table when the alarm went off."

Manny threw his hands in the air. "I swear, boss, I had access to the food, but I didn't do anything to it. I never even saw the guy until that night."

"Don't worry," Gallagher said, patting Manny on the back. "We know you didn't have a motive."

Manny breathed a sigh of relief. "That's good, because I don't need trouble finding me right now."

"I just had a thought," Connie said. "Manny, you said that Fernando was surprised to see Arnold Burton and his friends walk into the restaurant."

"That's right. A gentle wind could have blown him over."

"So, if Fernando *did* murder Arnold, it couldn't have been premeditated. He would have to have used something that was already in the restaurant.

Hopefully, the tests that the police are running on Arnold's salad will come back from the lab quickly. We need to know what Arnold was poisoned with to see if it's something Fernando would have had access to in the kitchen. If it's not, then Fernando must be innocent."

"True," Gallagher said. "If the poison that killed Arnold wasn't something commonly found in a restaurant, Fernando couldn't have done it."

Manny brightened up. "That's a good point."

Gallagher stood to leave, and Connie and Stephanie followed him.

"Thanks for your help, Manny," Gallagher said as Manny walked them to the door. "We're going to get this case solved ASAP so we can all get back to work."

"I hope so," Manny said. "I have a couple weeks' salary in my savings account, but after that I'll be up a creek without a paddle."

"I give you my word," Gallagher said.

They drove in silence for most of the way back to Stephanie's house. It wasn't until they got off Route 75 and were nearly on Sapphire Beach Boulevard that Connie broke the silence.

"We've got to find out who this woman is. We need to know if she is the one who set off the alarm, and if so, did she have a motive to kill Arnold?"

"Hopefully, Fernando can tell us more. When would you like to talk to him?" Gallagher asked.

"I've got to get back to the shop now, but how about tomorrow morning after Grace arrives? She usually gets there about 10:30 on Sundays, so that will give us about an hour before the store gets busy."

"Sounds good," Gallagher said. "Fernando lives in Sapphire Beach, so it shouldn't take too long. We'll pick you up at 10:45."

They exited Gallagher's car, and he and Stephanie walked Connie to hers.

"We have to find the killer, Connie," Gallagher said. "You heard Manny. My employees can't afford to be out of work for too long. And for that matter, neither can I."

Chapter 6

AFTER STOPPING BY her condo to pick up Ginger, Connie arrived at *Just Jewelry* in barely enough time to help Grace with the late Saturday morning rush, which kept them both on their toes until Grace's shift ended at 2:00.

A couple of hours later, while Connie was helping a customer choose a birthday gift for a friend, Abby raced into the store, breathless. She stopped abruptly as soon as she entered the shop and peered through the window. She looked to the right towards the beach, then to the left, and finally breathed a sigh of relief.

"I'll be right back," Connie said to the woman she was assisting.

"Is everything okay, Abby?"

Abby looked as though she were fighting back tears.

"I think so." She took a deep breath. "I mean, yes. I just have an overactive imagination, that's all. I must be reading too many mystery books."

Another group of customers came into the store, and the woman Connie had been helping was ready to make her purchase, so Connie didn't have a chance to press Abby for a better explanation. She also didn't want to upset Abby in front of customers.

"We'll talk later, when we're alone," Connie said.

"Honestly, I'm fine."

For the next hour, while they were each occupied with customers, Connie periodically glanced over at Abby. She was doing her best to stay focused on her job, but she wasn't her calm, cheerful self.

As soon as the foot traffic died down, Abby asked Connie if she could run out and grab some dinner.

Something told Connie that Abby was avoiding her.

"Of course," Connie said. "But I was hoping we could chat about what's going on. You don't seem like yourself."

Abby picked up her purse and fumbled through it, as if looking for something.

Connie put her hand under Abby's elbow, and Abby leapt back.

"I know something is wrong. Please tell me what it is."

Abby slung her purse over her shoulder. "Honestly, it's nothing. I forgot to eat lunch, so I guess I'm a bit jumpy. Low blood sugar can do that."

Connie had seen Abby skip meals before, and it never had *this* affect. "Okay, Abby, go ahead and grab some dinner. But if you change your mind and want to talk about it, I'm here."

Abby smiled nervously and dashed out the door.

When she returned a half hour later, she seemed much calmer.

"I just had a burger at a restaurant down the street. Thanks for covering for me. I think that did the trick."

Connie couldn't disagree. Abby did seem like her old self again.

"I miss Gallagher's sandwiches, though," Abby said. "I hope he can reopen soon."

"I agree. It's so depressing to look across the street and see the restaurant dark and empty. The street is usually alive with activity."

"Not to mention the yellow tape strung across the entrance," Abby added. "It's kind of creepy."

Although Connie had considered taking the evening off once the downtown streets started to clear out, she opted to stay until closing time to keep Abby company. She also hoped Abby might eventually confide in her about whatever was going on.

But no such luck.

At the end of the night, Connie walked with Abby to the parking lot at the end of the street, where they had both left their cars, just to be on the safe side.

Then she went home, took a leisurely walk with Ginger, and called it an early night.

On Sunday morning, after attending the 7:00 Mass at Our Lady, Star of the Sea Parish, Connie swung by her condo to pick up her four-legged bestie and made the one-mile commute down Sapphire Beach Boulevard to work.

Grace arrived at 10:30 with two coffees in hand, as was her habit after going to a later Mass, and the two chatted as they sipped their javas.

"I hate it when Stephanie gets involved in these investigations," Grace said. "It means that I have two of you to worry about now. But I understand why Gallagher is so anxious to get his restaurant back up and running."

"My heart breaks for him," Connie said. "Not to mention his employees, who need to earn a living."

Grace frowned. "I hope all the stress doesn't negatively impact his and Stephanie's relationship. It's still relatively new."

"I suppose it will be a trial, but my money is on them getting stronger as a result. Gallagher's a survivor. He'll be back up and running in no time, especially with Stephanie by his side."

"Speak of the devils," Grace said as Gallagher and Stephanie arrived to pick up Connie for their visit with Fernando.

"Promise me you'll be careful," Grace said. "I know it's important to find the killer, but it's not worth your lives."

Stephanie hugged her mother. "We promise."

Gallagher put his arm around Stephanie. "I won't let anything happen to her."

"You'd better not," Grace said. She clenched her fist. "I love you, but I'll knock you to the moon if anything happens to her."

"You wouldn't have to," Gallagher said. "I'd do it myself first."

Gallagher drove Connie and Stephanie to Fernando's house, which was in a trailer park ten minutes from downtown. "I called him last night to tell him I'd be coming over, so he'll definitely be home," he said.

They parked across the street, then followed the cement walkway to the door of a white trailer. Before Gallagher had a chance to knock, Fernando opened the door.

"I didn't realize you were bringing guests," he said, shifting from one foot to the other. "It's a little tight in here. Why don't we go for a walk?"

Before they could answer, Fernando had shut the door behind him. "The beach is right across the street. Let's head there."

Fernando already knew Stephanie, so Gallagher introduced him to Connie. "Connie has a talent for solving crimes, so I asked her to help us figure out what happened on Friday night. That way, we can all get back to work."

"Oh, this is the one you're always talking about," Fernando said.

Connie glanced at Gallagher, who was suppressing a smirk.

They found a secluded area at the beach where they sat down to talk. It was barely 11:00, and the sun was shining brightly in the turquoise sky. The sunny, tranquil morning stood in contrast to what Connie was feeling as she observed the concerned expression on Gallagher's face. This would be a tough conversation for him.

"As Gallagher said, the sooner this case is solved, the quicker the restaurant will be back up and running, so we are talking to everyone who might have seen anything on Friday night," Connie said.

Fernando, who was wearing faded blue jeans and a white t-shirt, pulled his legs against his chest. "And you figured that I'm the only guy with a record who had access to the victim's salad, so I must be the one who did it."

"It's not like that, Fernando," Gallagher said. "You were in a position to have possibly seen something important, and we want to know everything you know. That's all." Gallagher took a deep breath. "Okay, maybe that's *not* all. I also heard that you worked at *Seaview Restaurant* and were let go because of a complaint Arnold made. It must have been shortly after that that you were arrested."

"I've always been honest with you about my incarceration," Fernando said. "I even came clean to you about my gambling problem, even though I didn't have to. I've been on the straight and narrow since I got out of jail."

"I know. And I admire you for trying to make a better life for yourself. You are a hard worker and a talented cook."

Fernando sat up straighter after receiving Gallagher's compliment. "Honestly, I didn't want to lie to you about that other job, but you didn't know me yet. If I had told you I was fired for being a bad cook, would you have hired me as your head cook?"

Gallagher shrugged.

"That other restaurant was fancy," Fernando continued. "Who wants to cook like that, anyway?

Gallagher's Tropical Shack is more my speed. We serve real food with portions meant for hungry human beings, not rabbits."

"You've certainly found your niche as a cook in my restaurant," Gallagher said.

Fernando looked down at the sand. "Am I fired, boss?"

Gallagher crossed his arms and looked directly at Fernando. "Did you kill Arnold?"

"Of course not. The guy was a creep, but I didn't kill him."

"You know what they say, innocent until proven guilty," Gallagher said. "But I need you to be honest with me about something. Manny said you insisted on making the salad, even though that was Manny's job, and that you watched Arnold intently as he ate it."

"Oh, man, why did Manny have to go and tell you that?"

"So, it's true?" Gallagher asked.

"Yeah, it's true. But it's not what it seems like. I made the salad because I wanted to redeem myself. I watched Arnold eat it, because I wanted to see for myself that he enjoyed it and to prove to myself that he was wrong about me as a cook. That's all. Sure, seeing him brought up some bad memories, but I wouldn't have poisoned the guy. I wanted the personal satisfaction of making him the best darn salad he'd ever eaten. In hindsight, I'm glad I did, because it turned out to be his last meal."

"Did you notice anything unusual that night that might be helpful for us to know?" Connie asked.

Fernando shook his head. "Nothing at all. I was just as surprised as everyone else when it happened."

"There's one more very important question we have to ask you. We heard that a woman wandered into the kitchen on Friday night shortly before the alarm went off," Connie said.

"Yeah, that's right. She was looking for the ladies' room, so I showed her where it was."

"Do you know anything about her at all?" Connie asked. "We'd like to track her down and talk to her."

"That's a tough one. I asked her for her number, but she refused. I did get a first name, though. It was Priscilla. I saw her this morning at a coffee shop in a shopping center on the boulevard, but she still wouldn't give me the time of day. It's probably for the best. She was beautiful but a little snooty, if you ask me. It never would have worked between us."

"Which coffee shop did you see her at?" Connie asked.

"*Joseph's Java*."

"And what time were you there?"

"About 9:00."

They thanked Fernando for his time and walked him back to his home.

"I hope you guys find out who the killer is," Fernando said. "The police treated me like a suspect on Friday night, but I swear I didn't do it. I may have a motive, but it's a weak one, if you ask me. And it's not like we keep poison in the kitchen."

Fernando made a valid point.

"We'll do everything in our power," Connie assured him.

Chapter 7

GALLAGHER AND STEPHANIE brought Connie back downtown after their conversation with Fernando.

Gallagher pulled into a parking spot a short distance from *Just Jewelry* and turned his body so that he could see Stephanie, who was in the passenger seat, and Connie, who was in the back. "After talking with Evan, Manny, and Fernando, who's at the top of your list of suspects?"

"Besides Manny, there are at least five people who could have poisoned Arnold's salad - Dom, Ronnie, Kendra, Fernando, or Priscilla. Every one of them had the opportunity, and every one of them, with the possible exception of Priscilla, had a motive."

"We need to find Priscilla, like, yesterday," Gallagher said.

"Whoever she is," Stephanie added.

"Fernando could have killed Arnold in an act of revenge," Connie said. "But I think that's the most unlikely scenario. He didn't know Arnold was coming into the restaurant Friday night, and I doubt you keep anything in the kitchen that Fernando could have used to poison him. It's more likely that Dom, Ronnie, or Kendra wanted Arnold out of the picture so Kendra could purchase the tennis magazine."

"The question is, who has the most to lose if the sale doesn't happen?" Stephanie wondered aloud.

Gallagher seemed to relax. "It makes me feel better that Fernando isn't our top suspect."

"I don't like that he insisted on making Arnold's salad, or that he was watching Arnold as he ate it. But he did seem sincere," Connie said. "He's either caught in the middle of an unfortunate coincidence, or he's playing us big time."

"Dom is my top suspect," Gallagher said. "But, of course, we haven't talked to any of his colleagues yet, including Kendra."

"I'll see if I can find out from Evan where Kendra is staying," Stephanie said.

"Perfect," Connie said. "That sounds like a good next step. And we need to figure out who this Priscilla is. Who takes off in the middle of a fire alarm if they don't have something to hide?"

"*Joseph's Java* is right down the street from my new place," Gallagher said. "Fernando said he saw Priscilla there at 9:00 this morning, so she probably either lives or works in the area. I'm going to make it a point to hang out there for the next few mornings and see if I can find her. Since I'm not working, I have plenty of time on my hands."

"If she shows up, call me right away, and I'll meet you there if I can," Connie said.

"Will do."

"It sounds like we have a plan," Connie said, as she exited Gallagher's Nissan. We'll be in touch soon."

It was a madhouse when Connie returned to the store.

"The afternoon rush came early today," Grace said, as Connie sprang into action behind the cash register. By the time they got a reprieve a couple of hours later, they were both ready for a break, so Connie brewed a pot of strong iced tea.

Grace left shortly after and another rush of customers came through the door, which kept Connie on her toes until Abby arrived for her shift. Connie was relieved that Abby seemed to be back to her old self again.

About 6:00, Connie took Ginger for a quick walk, and when she returned, Zach was there.

"Perfect timing," Connie said, as she stepped out back to hang up the leash in the storage area.

When she returned, she joined him at the oak table.

"You look exhausted," Connie said. "Can I brew you a cup of coffee?"

Zach shook his head. "No thanks. I just wrapped up a long day, and I'm heading home. I plan to crash early, so caffeine would be counterproductive."

"How goes the investigation?" Connie asked.

"We got the results back from the lab earlier today. The victim's salad dressing was laced with arsenic. Now there's no doubt that Arnold was poisoned in Gallagher's restaurant."

"Does Gallagher know?"

Zach nodded. "Josh went to Stephanie's house this afternoon to give him the news in person. But that's not all. We found rat poison in a few of the corners of Gallagher's dining room and a half-empty package in the storage room. That means the killer didn't necessarily bring the arsenic into the restaurant. He or she could have used the rat poison to kill Arnold."

"So, the killer could be one of his employees," Connie said. That put Fernando back in the running.

"Gallagher swore he never would have brought rat poison into his restaurant," Zach said. "He insisted that he doesn't even have a rat problem."

"Maybe the killer planted it there to make it look like one of Gallagher's employees murdered Arnold," Connie suggested.

"That's what Gallagher thinks. But, anyway, I didn't come to talk about the case." Zach put his hand on Connie's. "It feels like ages since we've spent any time together."

"Well, unless you count me giving you my statement on Friday night as quality time."

Zach smiled. "Definitely not. I thought maybe we could move our date to Wednesday night instead of waiting until Friday. I know you usually work alone on Wednesday evenings, but I had something special planned, and I'd rather not wait until the weekend."

"I'd like that," Connie said, silently determining that she would not mention the change in plans to Elyse. After all, it *was* their second anniversary date, so Zach could have planned any number of ways to celebrate. This didn't necessarily mean that Elyse was right about a proposal. Did it?

"Let me see if Abby or Grace can cover for me."

Before Connie could even ask the question, Abby responded from behind the cash register. "No problem. I can cover for you. Especially if I can have a day off when my friend comes to town in a few weeks."

"Done deal," Connie said. "Thanks, Abby."

"How about if I pick you up at 6:45 at Palm Paradise?" Zach asked.

"That sounds good. Are we going to *White Sands Grill*, like we were supposed to on Friday?"

"Is that still your favorite restaurant?"

"It is. Especially at sunset."

"Perfect. Then that's where we'll go." As he kissed Connie and left, Zach's energy level seemed to rise a few notches.

Apparently, Abby noticed too. "It sounds like he has big plans for your date," she said after the door closed behind Zach. "Elyse might be right."

"I guess we'll see," Connie replied, feeling an energy spike of her own.

A few hours later, as Connie and Abby were getting ready to close the shop for the night, Gallagher and Stephanie popped in.

"I'm glad to see you two," Connie said. "Zach came in earlier. He filled me in on the arsenic in Arnold's salad dressing and the rat poison."

"It came as quite a blow," Gallagher said. "I swear, Connie, I would never bring rat poison into my restaurant. The killer had to have planted it."

"If that's the case," Connie said, "it had to be Fernando. Maybe he knew it was in the restaurant and took advantage of the situation to kill Arnold."

Gallagher released a deep sigh. "I suppose we can't rule that out, but my money is still on Ronnie, Dom, or Kendra, since they all had the strongest motives."

"Are you sure you're not letting your admiration for Fernando color your perspective?" Stephanie asked.

"I'll admit that I'm rooting for the guy. I saw something special in him when I hired him, and I still don't think I was wrong."

"You could be right. Sometimes it pays to listen to your gut," Connie said.

"Usually, my gut just tells me when I'm hungry, but in this case, I think it could be telling me something more useful," Gallagher said.

Connie chuckled. "Don't underestimate yourself. You have good instincts about people."

"He does," Stephanie agreed. "But he also has a huge heart. He might have seen in Fernando the qualities he wanted to see, and not what was there."

"Either way, we still have a lot of people to talk to," Connie said. "Kendra and Priscilla for starters. I know you're trying to strategically run into Priscilla in *Joseph's Java,* and hopefully Evan will know how to get in touch with Kendra."

"Funny you should mention that," Gallagher said. "My quick-thinking girlfriend took care of it already."

Stephanie smiled proudly.

"I noticed Evan walking to the beach this afternoon, so I asked him for Kendra's address." Stephanie pulled a slip of paper from her pocket and waved it in the air. "It's right here. She's actually renting a condo in Palm Paradise."

"Abby and I were just about to close up shop," Connie said. "Do you want to stop by tonight?"

"Isn't it kind of late to pop in on someone we don't know?" Stephanie asked.

"Under normal circumstances, I would agree," Gallagher said. "But desperate times call for desperate measures. I just finished speaking with some of my servers, and they are really stressed about being out of work. Some of them are already looking for another job. I can't blame them. It's not easy living from paycheck to paycheck, but if I have to hire and train all new help once I reopen, it will take even longer to get back on my feet."

Connie hated to see so much weight on Gallagher's shoulders, especially after things had finally begun to go his way. Gallagher had struggled with drug addiction when he was younger and had also briefly been involved with a cult. *Gallagher's*

Tropical Shack was the realization of his long-time dream to own a restaurant near the beach. During the restaurant's infancy stages, Gallagher invested most of his profits back into his business, driving a beat-up old car and living in a tiny trailer. Things had finally begun to go his way, and then this happened. Gallagher was right. Desperate times called for desperate measures.

"Okay," Connie said. "Let's give it a try."

They took separate cars to Palm Paradise and dropped Ginger off at Connie's place before going downstairs to the sixth floor, where Kendra's rental was located.

Gallagher knocked on the door, and shortly after, they were greeted by an attractive blond woman with an athletic build who appeared to be in her mid-forties. Connie immediately recognized her from *Gallagher's* on Friday night. Judging from her freshly applied makeup, she was on her way out.

"Can I help you?" the woman asked.

"My name is Connie. Are you Kendra?" Connie asked, even though she knew it was Kendra. She decided not to mention that she lived upstairs, in case the woman was dangerous.

Kendra studied the three of them for a moment. "Aren't you Gallagher? You own the restaurant where Arnold died, don't you?"

"That's right. We were hoping we could talk to you about what happened on Friday night."

"I really don't see what there is to talk about. I've told the police everything I know about Arnold and recounted everything I saw. I understand your business is at stake," she said to Gallagher, "but it doesn't seem prudent to be poking around a murder investigation."

If Connie had a dollar for every time she'd heard that, she'd be a wealthy woman.

"As you said, my livelihood and that of my employees is at stake. We just want to ask you a few questions."

"You might know more than you think," Connie added. "We wouldn't ask if so much weren't on the line."

Kendra smiled curtly. "Well, I am a businesswoman myself, so I guess I can understand your predicament. I suppose I could spare a few minutes."

She opened the door wider to let them in and led them to the dining room table, which was only a few steps away.

"How did you know Arnold?" Connie asked.

"As a tennis pro myself, I followed both of his careers - his time in the tennis tournament circuit, and, later with the magazine."

"We understand you were attempting to purchase *Tennis Times*," Connie said.

"Yes, that's right. But Arnold didn't want to sell. The magazine provided him with a lifestyle that he wasn't ready to part with, even though it would have been in his best financial interest to accept my offer. I even offered Arnold a job at the magazine, so he could have the best of both worlds. He would have been able to pocket a hefty sum from the sale of the magazine, plus earn a salary working for me and maintain his coveted lifestyle. But he made it clear he wouldn't work for someone else. If he couldn't be an owner, he didn't want any part of the magazine." She shook her head. "He was a good tennis player but a lousy businessman. It was undoubtedly Ronnie's and Dom's expertise that made the magazine a success."

"Evan told us that you are a persistent woman," Connie said.

"Did he? Well, I suppose that's true. I've been trying to purchase that magazine ever since I heard rumblings that Ronnie and Dom wanted to sell. I did everything in my power to change Arnold's mind." She looked directly at Gallagher. "But if you're thinking I killed him over a magazine, you're crazy."

"You are obviously very determined," Connie said. "You came to Sapphire Beach during the same two weeks as Arnold and his group."

"It's not like I'm here to stalk them. I came primarily to watch some tennis matches that were taking place in the area this month. Arnold being in town was just icing on the cake."

"But you took advantage of the situation to try to get Arnold to change his mind about selling," Gallagher said.

"As I said, I'm a businesswoman."

"Just one last question," Connie said. "You were seated at Arnold's table when the fire alarm went off. Did you see anything unusual during that time?"

Kendra shook her head. "I've been going over those few minutes in my mind since Friday night. I can't think of a single thing. The fire alarm sounded shortly after I was seated, and that distracted everyone, myself included. I wasn't paying attention to Arnold's food, and I doubt the people around me were, either."

Kendra stood up. "I don't mean to be rude, but I really do have to get going. I have plans, and I'm running late as it is."

They thanked Kendra for her time as she walked them to the door.

Connie paused and turned around before leaving. "I assume you'll be moving forward with purchasing the magazine now."

"It looks that way. But before you draw any hasty conclusions, the proceeds of the magazine will now be split two ways between Dom and Ronnie, rather than three. Arnold had no heirs. I know it sounds cold, but the fact is, Ronnie and Dom are the ones who will benefit the most from Arnold's death."

"And between the two of them, who seemed the most eager to sell?" Connie asked.

"Definitely Dom," Kendra said. "I understand he'll be using most of his profits to pay off a hefty gambling debt."

Chapter 8

AFTER THEY LEFT KENDRA'S apartment, Gallagher and Stephanie accompanied Connie upstairs to her condo to pick up Ginger so they could talk while Connie took her for her nightly walk.

They walked down the long driveway flanked with coconut palms, then took a right onto Sapphire Beach Boulevard, heading in the opposite direction from downtown, where it was quieter.

"What did you guys think about our conversation with Kendra?" Stephanie asked, as they crossed the boulevard toward the adjacent streets.

"Both Kendra and Evan suggested that Dom had more to gain from the sale of the magazine than Ronnie did," Connie said.

"I noticed that, too," Gallagher said. "I also noticed that Kendra, Dom, and Ronnie are already talking business, and Arnold has barely been dead for forty-eight hours."

"That *is* disturbing," Connie said. "And I hate to further complicate things, but three people stood to benefit from Kendra buying that magazine. It's possible that Ronnie, Dom, and Kendra were working together."

"Or two out of the three," Stephanie added.

They stopped to give Ginger a minute to sniff a Bougainvillea shrub that climbed a stucco wall in front of a Spanish-style house, then Connie tugged on the leash and they continued their walk.

Gallagher let out a frustrated sigh. "You're right, Connie. We need more information to go on. I'm trying to be as impartial as I can, because I'd be crushed if Fernando were guilty, but I really hope it wasn't him. I don't know how I would live with myself if I hired a murderer."

"Let's try not to think about that right now," Connie said. "He's only one of five suspects at the moment."

All of a sudden, Gallagher stopped walking. "I just had a horrible thought. What if Priscilla doesn't exist, and Fernando made her up just to divert attention away from himself? He knows I'll be checking *Joseph's Java* every morning. What if he's sending us on a wild goose chase?"

"But Manny also saw Priscilla, even though he didn't know her name," Connie said.

"I know. But he and Fernando have become good friends since they started working together. Manny could be covering for him," Gallagher said.

"They'd have to be extremely good friends for Manny to lie about a murder investigation," Stephanie pointed out.

"True," Gallagher said. "Manny wouldn't lie if he thought Fernando was guilty, but if he thought he was innocent, he might tell a white lie to protect his friend."

"I suppose that's a possibility, but I still think you should look for Priscilla." Connie said. "We need to stay focused and try not to imagine the worst."

"When I get back home, I'll search for her on the Internet," Stephanie said. "How many Priscillas could there be in Sapphire Beach who are young and have dark hair and blue eyes?"

"Don't forget, she could live in a nearby town and only *work* in Sapphire Beach," Connie said. "She could live in Fort Myers, Estero, Bonita Springs, or Naples. It would take a while to search all those towns."

"You're probably right, but I need to do something. I'll start with Sapphire Beach."

Gallagher squeezed Stephanie's hand. "I appreciate the help, but don't stay up too late. Tomorrow's a workday for you."

When they got back to Palm Paradise, Stephanie and Gallagher walked Connie into the lobby, then they left together.

Connie changed into her pjs and decided to watch some television before going to bed. As she was getting ready to call it a night, a group text came from Stephanie to Connie and Gallagher. *As far as I can tell, there is no Priscilla in Sapphire Beach who meets our Priscilla's description. She must live in another town.*

Gallagher replied first. *Thanks for trying, babe. Maybe I'll have better luck at the coffee shop. I'm going to set up camp there in the morning.*

On Monday morning, Kelly and Grace were already at *Just Jewelry* when Connie and Ginger arrived.

"Wow," Kelly said. "I leave work at 5:00 on Friday, and before I come in on Monday, you're already knee-deep in a murder investigation! I had a feeling it would be exciting working here, but I had no idea just *how* exciting."

When Connie didn't hear anything from Gallagher by 11:00, she figured that Priscilla didn't show up at *Joseph's Java* that morning. But, fortunately, Stephanie called to tell her that she ran into Evan before work and asked when a good time would be for them to try to talk with Dom and Ronnie. He informed her that they would all be attending a tennis match later that afternoon. Stephanie had to work and couldn't make it, but Gallagher planned to go.

"I'd like to be there," Connie said. "Let me see if I can get coverage in the store."

Kelly had only been working in *Just Jewelry* for a little over two months, and Connie hadn't left her alone in the store yet. But she really wanted to go to the tennis match at 2:00, and that was the time Grace left. She ran the idea past Kelly, who was confident that she would be fine alone for a couple of hours.

"You've taught me everything I need to know," Kelly said. "It will be a good practice run."

"The tennis match is right in town," Connie said. "I'll only be ten minutes away. If you need me, just call or text, and I'll come right back. I didn't want to leave you alone in the store until after Easter when it's slower, but I want to be there for Gallagher."

"I'd be happy to stay for a while," Grace said. "I know you're doing this to help Gallagher and by extension, Stephanie. I don't mind putting in a couple of extra hours. It would be my contribution to the case."

"I have an idea," Kelly said. "How about if you stay for an hour? Then you could leave, and I'd only be alone for one hour. It wouldn't quite be trial by fire that way."

"Just trial by a small flame," Connie said with a grin.

Gallagher picked Connie up at 1:45, and they drove to the Sapphire Beach Country Club, where the tennis match was taking place. Connie wore her fanciest sunglasses to blend in as much as possible amid the crowd sporting designer clothes and accessories.

Before choosing a seat, they stopped for a moment to scan the bleachers. Evan, who was sitting with Dom, Ronnie, and a few other people, including Kendra, gave them a curt nod.

Connie and Gallagher headed in their general direction. They tried to be discreet, but the annoyed glances that Ronnie and Dom exchanged with one another told Connie they had been spotted.

"It would be best if we could talk to each of them separately," Connie whispered to Gallagher, once they settled into their seats, which were only a short distance from Evan and the others. "We won't get as much information if they are together."

"Let's hang tight and wait for the right opportunity."

Connie and Gallagher waved at the others, as if they attended tennis matches on a regular basis. They did their best to clap at the appropriate times and to appear as interested as possible.

"I've been practicing the backhand that Evan taught me," Connie said. "Maybe if I stopped investigating murders, I'd have time to actually play."

"At least wait until after this one is solved before you give up your sleuthing habit," Gallagher said.

"Deal."

Connie and Gallagher periodically glanced behind them to see what Ronnie and Dom were doing. Finally, there was a brief intermission, and Ronnie stood up. "I'm going to get a cold beer," he said. "Does anyone else want something to drink?"

After the others put in their orders, Ronnie headed for the concession stand.

"I'll follow Ronnie," Gallagher said. "See if you can talk to Dom."

"It's going to be hard with his friends still there," Connie said. "I'll do my best."

Fortunately, Evan came to her rescue.

"Will you help me get something out of the car?" Evan asked his friends. "Dom, you stay here and save our seats."

He winked at Connie as he passed in front of her.

Connie ascended several bleachers and casually walked over to where Dom was sitting. He smirked as she approached him.

"If it isn't Sapphire Beach's resident amateur sleuth," he said. "I hear you're trying to beat the police in finding out what happened to Arnold."

"We're not trying to beat anybody. We just want justice for Arnold."

"And for your friend's restaurant to be able to reopen."

"Is that so bad?" Connie asked.

Dom smirked and looked away. "I can't say I blame you. But you're barking up the wrong tree here. Arnold was a good friend. I had nothing against him."

"Except for the fact that he refused to sell the magazine."

"That may be true, but you can't possibly believe I'd have killed him for *that*."

The conversation clearly wasn't going anywhere.

"I'm not accusing you of anything, Dom," Connie said. "But you did know Arnold well. Do you have any theories on what happened?"

"Well, I know *I* didn't do it, and if I thought Ronnie did, I wouldn't be staying in the same house as him."

Unless you both did it.

"I suppose that's true," Connie said. "Although, Ronnie doesn't have a motive to kill you, since you are in favor of selling the magazine. You weren't the one standing in his way."

"Perceptive," Dom said. "But really, why would I want to stay with someone who killed my business partner and friend? I would be long gone if I believed Ronnie was guilty."

"You must have a theory," Connie said. "There were only so many people at the restaurant who had a motive. What are your thoughts?"

Dom quickly scanned the area around them. "My money is on Kendra. She had her sight set on buying our magazine, and she is one determined woman. She was also in the perfect position to poison Arnold's food when the fire alarm went off."

"I suppose she could have killed Arnold so she could buy the magazine."

"She didn't want *Tennis Times* simply for business purposes. Arnold had a way of cutting people down, and he made sure Kendra knew that he didn't think she had what it took to run a successful magazine. He also once told Kendra at a table full of people that she might as well write about tennis, because she wasn't a good player. Kendra tried to pretend he didn't bother her, but she detested him."

"Enough to kill him?" Connie asked.

Dom shrugged. "That's the million-dollar question."

Chapter 9

CONNIE WAITED FOR GALLAGHER to return before going back to her seat.

When he and Ronnie arrived, Gallagher placed four plastic cups filled with beer on a bleacher and slapped Ronnie on the back. "Nice talking with you," he said. Then he and Connie returned to their seats. Connie was pretty sure she saw Dom roll his eyes at Ronnie as they left.

Connie and Gallagher watched about ten more minutes of the match, then decided to leave.

While they were driving back, Connie relayed her conversation with Dom.

"I don't trust him," she said. "Did you see Dom roll his eyes at Ronnie as we were leaving?"

"Yeah," Gallagher said. "But I pretended I didn't. I figured if he underestimates us, we can go all Columbo on him."

Connie laughed out loud, mostly at the idea of Gallagher in a beige trench coat. "I suppose you're right."

"I don't trust Ronnie, either," Gallagher said. "He did his best to avoid talking with me, but when I got in line at the concession stand, he had no choice, unless he wanted to risk having our conversation overheard. It was the only way I could get him to step away and talk."

"What did he say?" Connie asked.

"Basically, the same thing as Dom. He suspects Kendra, too, although he also thinks it could be Fernando. When I asked him about Dom's gambling debt, he confirmed that it was true. It seems Dom owes a lot of money, and he desperately needs the sale of the magazine to go through."

"Well, it looks like it will, now that Arnold's out of the picture," Connie said.

"Evan, Ronnie, and Kendra have all confirmed that Dom had the most to gain from Arnold's death," Gallagher said. "I think Dom is my top suspect."

"Agreed," Connie said. "Although Dom was right about one thing. For Kendra to follow them to Sapphire Beach in hopes of getting Arnold to change his mind about selling, she must really want the magazine."

"Kendra said that she came primarily to attend some tennis matches, but I don't think she's being entirely honest. I'll bet her primary motive was acquiring the magazine," Gallagher said.

Connie had to agree.

When Connie got back to *Just Jewelry,* Kelly was helping a woman choose a pair of earrings. There were a few other customers milling about, but Kelly seemed to have everything under control. She even gave Connie a thumbs up.

"How did it go?" Connie asked after the customers left.

"To be honest, I had butterflies after Grace left, but everything went smoothly. I was only alone for forty-five minutes."

"I never had a doubt," Connie said. "You've worked here during the busiest months, so you're well-prepared."

"True," Kelly said. "But I'm glad I'm easing into being left alone. It feels different when you're in charge."

The rest of the day flew by. Kelly left at 5:00, and Connie worked alone until closing time.

When she returned home for the evening, she threw on her fleece sweatshirt, since it was a cool evening, and took Ginger for a leisurely walk. Then she did some reading in bed until she fell asleep.

On Tuesday morning, as Connie was pouring her second cup of coffee, her cell phone rang. It was Gallagher.

"Hey, Gallagher, what's up?"

"Sorry to call you so early, but I've been sitting here at *Joseph's Java* since 7:00 this morning determined to find Priscilla, and I think she just walked in."

"Try to stall her. I'll be right there." Connie turned off her coffee pot and raced toward the door.

Ginger sat next to her leash, wagging her chestnut and white tail.

"I'll be back to get you on my way to work," Connie promised, scratching the top of Ginger's head.

Less than ten minutes later, Connie was peering through a window at *Joseph's Java.* Gallagher was sitting at a table in the corner of the cafe with a woman who fit Fernando's description of the mysterious Priscilla.

Connie took out her cellphone and opened the camera application. She entered the coffee shop, and, as discreetly as possible, aimed her phone at Priscilla and snapped a few pictures.

Then she walked over to the young woman, who appeared to be on the verge of tears.

"There's no reason to be afraid," Connie said, sitting next to Gallagher. "We just want to know what happened to Arnold Burton at Gallagher's restaurant on Friday night. It's Priscilla, right?"

The young woman nodded.

"Why were you in Gallagher's kitchen on Friday night?"

Her deep blue eyes darted between Connie and Gallagher. "It's like I told Gallagher. I was looking for the restroom. I guess I took a left when I should have taken a right at the bar. Anyway, one of the cooks showed me where it was located. He said he was heading there anyway, but I think he lied."

"What do you mean?" Gallagher asked. "Why would he lie about that?"

"It's just that he wouldn't stop complimenting my eyes and wanted my phone number. He came on so strong that it made me feel uncomfortable. I stayed in the restroom a few minutes longer than I needed to, hoping that he would be gone when I left."

"Priscilla, the fire alarm is right next to the restroom. Are you the one who set it off?"

"Yes. But you have to believe me, I didn't do it on purpose. I was so flustered over Fernando that I wasn't paying attention, and I backed into it and hit it with my elbow by accident."

"I'm sorry that you didn't feel comfortable in my restaurant," Gallagher said. "I'll definitely have a talk with Fernando about that. But why didn't you tell anyone that it was you who set off the alarm?"

Priscilla stared into her coffee. "I didn't see the point. The firefighters would have had to come, anyway, and I just wanted to get out of there, so I left. I figured they would see there was no fire, and you'd be able to open back up again."

"That's pretty much what happened," Connie said.

"But then, the next day, I heard that a man was murdered, and I panicked. I was afraid to call the police, because I heard the victim was poisoned and I knew I had been in the kitchen. I was afraid I would be a suspect. I should have gone to the police, but I was terrified."

"Priscilla, as long as you don't have a motive, you can't be a suspect," Connie said. "Had you ever met Arnold before?"

"Never. I heard he used to be a famous tennis player, but I don't follow tennis. I had no idea who he was until I read about him in an online article."

"When you were in Gallagher's kitchen that night, did you see anything unusual?" Connie asked.

"I don't think so. The men were cooking, that's all. I just remember that they looked as surprised to see me as I was to be in the kitchen. I didn't notice much besides that."

"What about at any other point while you were in the restaurant?" Connie asked. "Try to think. Did you see anything unusual at all? Whoever killed Arnold had to have been in the restaurant at that point."

Priscilla narrowed her eyes. "I don't think so. I remember looking around the dining room, because I was there to meet a friend, but she hadn't arrived yet. The only thing I remember is a waitress taking a picture of a group of friends sitting at a table near the back. But I didn't see anything unusual."

"I remember them," Gallagher said. "They were celebrating one of their twenty-fifth birthdays."

"You said their table was in the back of the restaurant?" Connie asked.

Priscilla and Gallagher nodded.

"Was it near Arnold's table?"

"Come to think of it, it was just a couple of tables away," Gallagher said. "You don't suppose they might have caught anything interesting in their photos?"

"That's what I was thinking. Do you remember if they paid with a credit card?"

"They did," Gallagher said. "Several, actually. They split the bill four ways. I remember because I rang up their purchase to save their server from having to take the time to divide the bill, since she was busy with her other tables. If I can get into my restaurant, I can probably get some names. With any luck, we can track down one or more of them."

Priscilla was beginning to fidget, and it was obvious that she was anxious to leave.

"Thank you for talking with us," Connie said. "I know you're afraid, but you really need to tell the police what happened. They need to know that it wasn't the killer who set off the alarm. That's an important piece of information, and they could be wasting precious time trying to figure it out."

Priscilla let out a deep sigh. "I hadn't thought of it that way. I guess you're right. I'll go to the police station right now."

Connie smiled. "I think that's a good idea."

"What do you think?" Gallagher asked Connie after Priscilla left.

"I'm glad she's going to the police. She might have seen something that could help them, even if she doesn't realize it. Unless she's lying, she doesn't seem to have any connection to Arnold." Connie pulled out her phone and opened the photo of

Priscilla she had taken. "When I was walking in, I snapped some photos of her."

"Great thinking!" Gallagher said.

"I want to show it to Evan and see if Arnold knew her, just to confirm that she has no connection to him. If she doesn't, she's probably telling the truth."

"Assuming she is telling the truth, it sounds like it wasn't the killer who sounded the alarm. If the alarm going off was a coincidence, then we're not necessarily looking for two killers. There's likely only one."

"You could be right," Connie said. "I'll text the photo to Stephanie so she can ask Evan if he recognizes Priscilla."

"And I'll ask Zach and Josh if I can gain access to my office so I can look through my receipts from Friday night. I'm sure I'll be able to recognize the receipts that belong to the folks who were taking pictures. Maybe with a little research, we can get a phone number, as well."

"Sounds like a plan," Connie said. "I'd better get going. I have just enough time to pick up Ginger before I have to get to the store."

Chapter 10

AFTER PICKING UP GINGER at her condo, Connie arrived at *Just Jewelry* a couple of minutes before opening time. Kelly was already there and was filling Ginger's water bowl in anticipation of the popular canine's arrival.

As she walked from the parking lot to her shop, Connie noticed that the yellow tape had been removed from the entrance to Gallagher's restaurant.

While they waited for customers to arrive, Connie texted Stephanie the photo of Priscilla that she had taken that morning so she could ask Evan if he had ever seen her before.

Then she filled Kelly in on her unexpected visit to *Joseph's Java* that morning.

"Do you think Priscilla was telling the truth?" Kelly asked.

"I tend to think she was. She seemed more like a scared kid than a killer."

"Or maybe she was afraid, because she killed Arnold and you and Gallagher managed to track her down," Kelly suggested.

"That's possible, but as far as we know, she doesn't have any connection to Arnold. We did manage to convince her to go to the police, so if she is lying, I'm sure they'll figure that out."

"That's good news. It sounds like it was a productive conversation."

"It was. Priscilla is at the bottom of my suspect list, now. We are not at a loss for people with a strong motive, so I'd rather focus on them."

"For Grace's sake, I hope you find the killer," Kelly said. "It's obvious how fond of Gallagher she is. I think she's hoping he and Stephanie will be together for a long time."

"I know. I hope they are, too."

A few customers were browsing some of the merchandise in the Fair Trade section, so Kelly went over to see if they needed help. Connie checked her phone, and there was a reply from Stephanie. *I will talk to Evan first thing tomorrow. I'm in Fort Myers right now. I had an early client this morning.*

That's perfect. It's not urgent. It's a long shot, but it's worth following up on.

In the meantime, how about if you, me, and Elyse meet at Surfside Restaurant *tonight for a girls' night out? I know you have to work until 9:00, but we could grab drinks and appetizers after that.*

That works for me. I'll text Elyse to see if she's free.

I already did, Stephanie replied. *We'll see you at* Surfside *at 9:30.*

Connie smiled as she threw her phone into her purse. It was nice to have something to look forward to.

It was a relatively slow day, so Connie spent much of it making jewelry, while Kelly tended to customers. Before Kelly left at 5:00, Connie took Ginger for a long walk around town, which served the dual purpose of giving Ginger some exercise and helping build Kelly's self-confidence about being in the store alone.

The evening was even slower than the afternoon, so when Zach called at 8:00, she was happy to have the distraction.

"Hi, Connie. I was hoping to be able to stop by in person before you closed tonight, but I'm swimming in work. I just wanted to confirm our dinner date for tomorrow evening. I made reservations at *White Sands Grill* for 7:00."

"I'm looking forward to take two of our anniversary date," Connie said.

"So am I."

It was shaping up to be a good week after all. First, *Surfside* tonight with her friends, and tomorrow a special date with Zach.

"I'll see you at Palm Paradise at 6:45," he said.

"I'll see you then. Wait... Zach?"

"Yeah, I'm still here."

"What did you think about Priscilla?"

"Priscilla who?"

"The young woman who set off the fire alarm at *Gallagher's* on Friday night."

"I have no idea what you're talking about, Connie. I know Fernando talked to a woman named

Priscilla, but I don't know anything about a fire alarm. What did you hear?"

"Gallagher and I talked to her this morning. She told us she accidentally set off the alarm when she was coming out of the ladies' room on Friday night. She promised she would go to the police station to talk to you this morning."

"She never came," Zach said. "This is the first I've heard about her setting off the alarm."

Connie described Priscilla to Zach and texted him the photo she had taken. "I think she regularly goes to *Joseph's Java.* Maybe you can catch her there in the morning."

"I'll send someone over, but if she's trying to avoid us, I doubt she'll be going back. But thanks for the information. I'll see you tomorrow," Zach said.

While Connie was straightening up, she noticed a light on inside *Gallagher's Tropical Shack*. Since the yellow crime scene tape had been removed, it probably wasn't the police, so she quickly texted Gallagher to make sure he knew someone was in there.

Gallagher's reply came quickly. *Yeah, it's me. Thanks for checking. Josh gave me permission to access my computer, so I'm here looking through credit card slips to see if I can find the names of the people who were taking photos on Friday night.*

Awesome, Connie replied. *Keep me posted.*

Will do. Have fun tonight. Stephanie said you are getting together at Surfside.

Connie replied with a smiley face emoji.

The second it turned 9:00, Connie brought Ginger back to Palm Paradise, took her for a quick walk, and headed back downtown to meet her friends at *Surfside Restaurant*. They were already seated at an outdoor table when Connie arrived.

"You two are a sight for sore eyes," Connie said. "It's been so hectic between training Kelly during the busy season, and with everything going on with Gallagher, I've barely had time to do anything fun since Sam left in January."

Their favorite server, Mandy, came to take their drink order. They each ordered a frozen cocktail, as well as nachos, spring rolls, and chicken tenders to share. Connie also ordered a bowl of French onion soup, since she hadn't eaten dinner yet.

"I was going to call you earlier to tell you something, but I knew you were alone in the store, so I figured I'd wait until tonight," Stephanie said after their drinks arrived.

Connie took a sip of her frozen Margarita. "Tell me what?"

"When I got home from work today, there was a note under my door from Evan. It said that he had important information regarding the case, and he asked if we could meet at 5:00 tomorrow at my house. He also said he wanted to ask us a question. He told me to leave a note with my response in my mailbox. I just talked to Gallagher, and he said he could make it."

"Zach's picking me up at 6:45 for our date, so I could probably make the meeting and still have enough time to get ready."

"Don't even think about it," Stephanie said. "Gallagher and I can handle this one alone. After all, we learned from the master. You just focus on your date."

"I suppose it's time to set you two loose in the world of amateur sleuthing. It's a proud moment for me," Connie said, putting her hand on her chest to dramatize the moment.

"I feel like there should be a diploma involved," Stephanie said with a chuckle.

"I'll get right on that," Connie said. Then she playfully wagged her index finger at Stephanie. "And don't forget to show Evan the photo of Priscilla, or there'll be no diploma. I talked with Zach tonight, and he told me that Priscilla never showed up at the police station to tell them about the fire alarm, as she promised us she would."

"We won't forget," Stephanie said. "But that's not a good sign. It makes it look like she's hiding something."

"She might have just gotten scared again," Connie said. "We'll have a better sense once you show Evan the picture."

Connie and Stephanie spent a few minutes catching Elyse up on the rest of the details of the case, since she hadn't been in the loop.

"Josh has been working nonstop this week," Elyse said. "The only reason I was able to come out tonight is that Zach is covering for him so he could spend some time with our daughters. Josh is returning the favor by working tomorrow night so Zach can take you out for your anniversary date."

"That's why Zach called earlier. He wanted to confirm our plans and let me know that he made reservations again at *White Sands Grill*. I'm looking forward to a nice dinner in a romantic setting."

Elyse smiled playfully. "Josh said that Zach has been walking on air the past couple of weeks. I think he's going to pop the question."

Connie rolled her eyes. "Here we go again."

"Okay, I'll stop. Just promise you'll call me as soon as you get home, especially if there's any big news."

"Don't forget about me," Stephanie said.

"You will both be one of the first to know." A nostalgic smile spread across Connie's face.

"What is it?" Elyse asked.

"I was recently reminiscing with my sister about my first date with Zach."

"That was an epic first date," Elyse said. "You went parasailing and had a monumental breakthrough in Natasha's case."

Natasha had owned a boutique in the building that now housed *Just Jewelry*.

"If you hadn't solved that case, we wouldn't have adopted Victoria," Elyse said. "I always remind Josh of that when he gets annoyed at your involvement in his cases."

"So, *that's* why he's been leaving me alone about that lately," Connie said. "I should have figured that out. But that's not what I meant. I was telling Gi about the night before our first date, when the three of us gathered at Stephanie's. I was freaking out, thinking I wasn't ready for a relationship, and the two of you calmed me down and convinced me to take it one step at a time."

"I remember that night," Stephanie said. "I forgot how nervous you were. And here we are, best friends, hanging out on a deck by the Gulf of Mexico the night before what could potentially be the biggest date of your life."

Elyse raised her half empty glass. "To our friendship. May we celebrate many more milestones together."

The women spent the rest of the evening reminiscing about the past two years. After a walk on the beach and a lot of laughter, they each headed home.

Chapter 11

ON WEDNESDAY MORNING, Connie sprung out of bed before her alarm went off, rejuvenated after an evening with her friends and excited for her date with Zach later that evening.

A steady flow of foot traffic kept Kelly and Grace busy all morning while Connie focused on some accounting paperwork. After Grace left, Connie and Kelly remained busy tending to customers until Abby arrived at 4:00.

When they saw Abby, Connie and Kelly exchanged a concerned glance.

"Abby, are you okay?" Connie asked.

"I'm fine. Why do you ask?"

"You look as if you haven't slept in weeks," Kelly said. "If you're sick, I can get my husband to watch Andy so you can take the night off."

"Or I can see if Grace is available," Connie suggested.

Abby waved away their concern. "I'm totally fine. I'm probably tired from all the late-night studying."

Connie looked skeptically at Abby. "After dinner, Zach and I will stop by the store to make sure you're okay."

"Don't you dare," Abby said. "I promise I'm fine. You should leave now and get ready for your big date."

"I'll keep an eye on her," Kelly said when Abby went out back to store her backpack. "If she doesn't get her energy back, I will either stay with her myself or call Grace."

"Thanks, Kelly. I really appreciate it. I'd hate to have to cancel this date with Zach."

Tonight, Connie was extra glad she decided to go ahead and hire a third employee.

With Kelly's reassurance, Connie left to get ready for her date. Before going upstairs, she took Ginger for a stroll along the boulevard, then hopped in the shower. After she got ready, she glanced at the time on her cable box. Zach wouldn't be there for another half hour, but Stephanie and Gallagher would probably be done with their meeting with Evan by now. She sat on her light blue tufted couch and called Stephanie to find out how the meeting went.

"Hi, Connie," Stephanie answered after one ring.

"Hey, Stephanie. I'm just waiting for Zach, so I thought I'd check in and see what big news Evan had to share with you."

"Gallagher and I are still sitting here on my front porch. We've been waiting for him since 4:30. We were going to knock on his door, but we decided against it because his note made it seem like he wanted to talk in private."

"That's probably smart. Maybe he couldn't break away from Dom and Ronnie," Connie said. "He'll probably come by later."

"Gallagher is staying for a while in case he does. We're just going to hang tight and watch a movie. Have fun tonight."

As they were talking, Elyse's name popped onto Connie's screen.

"Stephanie, I have to run. Elyse is calling in."

Stephanie chuckled. "She probably wants to talk about your date. Talk to you later."

Connie disconnected her call with Stephanie and accepted Elyse's call. "Elyse, Zach hasn't even picked me up yet, so I have no news," she said, before Elyse could get a word in.

"You may not have any news, but I do."

"What are you talking about?" Connie asked.

"I think your date with Zach is canceled. Evan was reported missing by his friend Ronnie. Josh and Zach are still at the police station talking to Ronnie."

Connie opened her mouth to speak but couldn't get any words to come out.

"Connie, are you there?"

"I'm here. That explains why Evan never showed up for his meeting with Gallagher and Stephanie. I don't know if I'm more shocked that Evan is missing or disappointed that my date with Zach is once again getting postponed."

Ginger hopped onto her lap and she stroked the spaniel's silky chestnut and white fur. Connie's body relaxed.

"I'm sorry to be the one to have to tell you," Elyse said. "Josh just called me. Zach is still in the interview room, and he's going to call you as soon as he can, but I told Josh I'd let you know right away. I'm so bummed."

Connie had to laugh. "You sound almost as disappointed as I am."

"I probably am. I wish I could stay on the phone, but I have to go. Emma had dinner at a friend's house, and I have to pick her up."

After she hung up with Elyse, Connie texted Stephanie to see if she and Gallagher were still at her house. *Zach had to cancel our date. It's a long story, but it's connected with the case. Can I stop by and explain to you and Gallagher in person?*

Of course. We're here, Stephanie replied.

Connie changed into casual clothes, then she and Ginger hopped in her silver Jetta and drove to Stephanie's bungalow, a short distance away.

"I hope you don't mind that I brought Ginger," Connie said when she arrived.

Stephanie bent down to greet the dog. "Of course not. I love this precious pup."

Stephanie brought a pitcher of iced tea and some fudge brownies out to her lanai, and they sat around the table.

"Thanks," Connie said. "I could use the pick-me-up."

"So, why did Zach cancel your date?" Gallagher asked.

"According to Elyse, late this afternoon Ronnie came to the police station to report Evan missing. Apparently, nobody has seen him for more than twenty-four hours."

"That explains why he didn't show up to our meeting," Gallagher said.

"I hope he's okay. What if the killer murdered Evan, because he was a threat to his or her identity?" Stephanie asked.

"What if he got hurt because the killer knew he planned to talk to us?" Gallagher asked.

"Let's not jump to conclusions," Connie said. "It's equally possible that Evan felt he was in danger and took it upon himself to disappear."

"I wish we knew what Evan wanted to tell us," Gallagher said.

"Me, too," Connie said. "I'll see what I can find out from Zach when he calls me tonight, and I'll let you know. Then we can regroup and figure out what our next move should be. In the meantime, I think I'll go back to *Just Jewelry*. Abby didn't look well when I left, so I'll feel better if I go and check on her."

"Sounds like a plan," Gallagher said. "We'll keep in touch."

"Hold on!" Stephanie said, as Connie was about to leave. She looked at Gallagher. "In all the excitement, we almost forgot to tell you."

"That's right," Gallagher said, pulling his phone from the pocket of his khaki shorts. "I was able to track down one of the guys who was with the group celebrating a birthday last Friday. He sent me these photos." Gallagher handed his phone to Connie, who scrolled through the pictures.

Most of them didn't seem to contain anything interesting - just some selfies and a couple of group pictures. Then Connie got to a picture of a couple. She enlarged the photo. Behind the couple, there was a clear shot of Arnold's table. Kendra was whispering something in Dom's ear.

"This one is interesting," Connie said.

"Kendra and Dom?" Gallagher asked.

Connie nodded.

"We thought so, too. It looks like they are conspiring about something."

"We need to ask Kendra and Dom about it," Connie said. "But right now, I'd better get going."

When Connie returned to *Just Jewelry*, Abby had just finished ringing up a customer.

"What on earth are you doing here?" Abby asked, when she saw Connie. "You don't look like you're dressed for your date. I thought Zach was taking you to *White Sands Grill*?"

For the second time that night, Connie explained what happened.

"I'm sorry about your date, but I hope Evan is okay," Abby said. "Do you think someone was afraid of what he might tell the police? Or you for that matter?"

"It's a strong possibility," Connie said.

"You didn't have to come here. You should take the night off to do some sleuthing. It's been a slow night, anyway."

"There's something more important I'd like to talk to you about," Connie said, gesturing for Abby to follow her to the seating area in the shop, since there were no customers. The downtown streets were emptying out, and it looked like foot traffic might be slow for the rest of the night.

Abby took a seat on the red sofa and Connie sat across from her on one of the armchairs.

"What's going on?" Abby asked.

"That's exactly what I wanted to ask you. I've noticed that you've been jumpy lately, and you don't look like you've had a good night sleep all week. As your friend, I'm concerned about you. I want you to level with me."

Abby took a deep breath. "I didn't realize it was that obvious. I should have known you'd pick up on it."

"Please tell me what's going on. You can trust me."

"It's not that I don't trust you. But it's probably all in my imagination," Abby said.

Connie waited for Abby to continue.

"It started last week. I was running errands in town before a shift, and I had the feeling someone was following me. When I looked around, I didn't see anyone, but the feeling lingered. I don't know who it could be."

"I remember noticing that you were jumpy before Arnold's murder, so it can't be connected to that."

"It's definitely not. I was inside helping customers when the whole thing happened at *Gallagher's*, so I couldn't possibly have inadvertently witnessed anything. And you're right. It started a few days before that. The first time I didn't think anything of it. But it's happened several times. It's a creepy feeling. I don't like it."

"Do you want me to go with you to talk to the police about it?" Connie asked.

Abby adamantly shook her head. "Please, no. It could be nothing, and I don't see what the police could do about it, anyway. Hopefully, it's all in my imagination and will pass."

"Okay, Abby, I understand where you're coming from. But promise me that you'll be extra vigilant, and if you feel you are in danger, you'll call Zach or at least tell me, and we can call him together."

"Thanks, Connie. I feel better already. My friend has been crashing at my place this week, so I don't have to be alone, but I don't know how long she'll be willing to do that."

"I have a guest room, so if she leaves and you don't feel comfortable staying by yourself, just let me know. Grace has a guest room, too, and our building is very secure. Promise you'll stay with one of us if you don't feel safe."

Abby hugged Connie. "I promise. Thank you."

"Just to be on the safe side, I'm going to stay here until closing time tonight."

"That's totally not necessary," Abby said. "I feel safe here. There are shops and people all around us. Nothing could happen in here."

"You're probably right, but I think I'll hang out anyway and make some jewelry. I'm just waiting to hear from Zach, so I might as well stay productive."

"I'll join you at the table and do some reading for class until our next customer comes in," Abby said.

A few minutes later, Connie received a text from Zach. *I'm so, so sorry about tonight. I'll call you as soon as I can. Hopefully, we can reschedule for the weekend.*

I understand, Connie replied. *Miss you, but we'll talk soon.*

As Connie and Abby were getting ready to close the shop, Zach called. "I'm wrapping up at work for the night. Where are you?"

"I'm at the shop. Abby and I are just about to close."

"Okay. I'd really like to see you tonight. Can I meet you at your place in a half hour?"

Connie smiled. "I'll be there. See you when you get there."

Chapter 12

AFTER BRINGING GINGER for her nightly walk, Connie went upstairs and waited for Zach. Her rumbling stomach reminded her that she only had a fudge brownie for dinner, so she put some leftovers from a few nights ago into the oven. She made enough for Zach, too, assuming he probably hadn't eaten yet, either.

"Something smells good," Zach said, when he walked into her condo.

"Nothing fancy. Just some meatloaf, mashed potatoes, and peas from the other night. I figured you probably skipped dinner, too, so I heated up plenty."

They each made themselves a plate and took their food into the living room, where Connie set up two TV trays.

After they said the blessing, Zach looked at Connie and smiled. But his eyes betrayed his disappointment. "I'm sorry we had to cancel our date again. But it's nice to be here with you at the end of a long day."

"What happened with Evan was beyond anyone's control," Connie said.

"I know. But still... You went out of your way to get coverage in your store, and I had something special planned. Would it be okay if we reschedule for Saturday?"

"That works for me. You know what they say. The third time's a charm."

Zach held her gaze. "I hope so."

"So, do you have any idea what happened to Evan?" Connie asked.

"We're still investigating. Ronnie came to the police station late this afternoon and told us that Evan never came home last night and that neither he nor Dom had seen him since the previous afternoon. The three of them are sharing a rental car for the week, which is still in the driveway. According to both Ronnie and Dom, Evan didn't mention that he was going anywhere. Neither of them has any idea where Evan could be."

"Have you talked to Kendra?"

"We've questioned everyone who Evan has been in contact with since he's been in Sapphire Beach. Nobody, including Kendra, admits to having seen him in the past twenty-four hours. Kendra doesn't really have a motive to want Evan out of the picture," Zach said. "He had no say over the sale of the magazine."

"Unless Kendra killed Arnold and Evan had proof."

Zach put down his fork. "Why would you say that? Did something happen to lead you to believe that Evan knew who the killer was?"

Connie hesitated. "Well, we're not sure if it's connected to his disappearance, but Evan left a note on Stephanie's door saying that he had some news for us. He was supposed to meet us this evening, but obviously he never showed up."

"But we were supposed to be on a date," Zach said. "How were you going to meet with Evan?"

“I wasn’t. Stephanie and Gallagher were planning to meet him without me.”

Zach leaned back in his armchair. “You should have told me this right away. It would have been useful to have that information. Not to mention that you could have put yourselves in a dangerous situation. What if Evan had told you something incriminating, and the killer came after you?”

“I think if Evan had anything solid, he would have gone directly to you or Josh.”

“Still,” Zach said. “With Evan now missing, the danger just escalated. The three of you need to be extra vigilant, especially Stephanie. She might be living next door to a killer.”

“Do you think Ronnie or Dom killed Arnold?”

“It’s a strong possibility. Oh, and this morning we tracked down Priscilla. She said she had been planning to come to us and tell us everything later today.”

“Do you believe her?”

“I doubt she had any intention of talking to us, but so far, we haven’t found any connection between her and Arnold. She doesn’t seem to have a motive.”

"At least now you know who set off the alarm. If Priscilla isn't the killer, it looks like it was a lucky coincidence for the real killer that she accidentally caused all that confusion. She may have inadvertently helped him or her to commit murder."

"She seems to realize that," Zach said. "That might be why she didn't want to tell us. I think she feels guilty about it. I tried to assure her that whoever killed Arnold probably would have succeeded either way. She's just a scared college student who lives at home with her parents."

It still didn't sit right with Connie that Priscilla didn't come forward with the information she had, especially since she promised she would.

When they finished eating, they straightened up the kitchen, and Connie walked Zach to the door.

"So, same plan for Saturday night?" Connie asked.

"I'll pick you up here at 6:45. I don't care how many crimes take place on Saturday. This time, we are having that date!"

He kissed her and left.

Since there was nothing good on television, Connie went to bed.

A few minutes after Connie, Grace, and Kelly opened the shop on Thursday morning, Gallagher and Stephanie stopped in.

"We just came by to see if you learned anything from Zach last night," Gallagher said.

"Aren't you working today?" Connie asked Stephanie.

She took Gallagher's hand. "I took today and tomorrow off. I thought Gallagher could use some moral support."

"I almost forgot," Grace said. "How was your anniversary date?"

They filled Kelly and Grace in on Evan's disappearance the previous day.

"That's awful," Grace said. "And it's too bad about your date. Isn't that the second time your anniversary date was canceled?"

"Yup," Connie said. "But Zach came by my condo last night after work and we rescheduled for this weekend. He said it was as if Evan just dropped off the face of the earth."

"I have a feeling Dom or Ronnie found out Evan was talking to us," Gallagher said. "Or at least that he knew something about the case that might incriminate one of them."

"I agree," Stephanie said. "Evan disappeared shortly after he left the note on my door."

"It could be," Connie said. "Zach also said that he tracked down Priscilla and was able to question her."

"What did he think about her?" Stephanie asked.

"He thinks she's just a scared kid. But it bothers me that she withheld information in a murder investigation. I still say she might be hiding something. Zach said she is a student. Let me see if I can find her. She probably goes to Florida Sands." Connie pulled out her laptop and did an Internet search for 'Priscilla Florida Sands University.'"

A social media page popped up with Priscilla's profile picture.

"Here we go," Connie said. She skimmed the content of Priscilla's page. "Bingo. She works at *Chic Boutique*."

"That's in the same shopping center as *Joseph's Java*. That explains why she goes there for coffee," Gallagher said.

"She seems to stop there in the morning," Connie said. "Maybe she's working now."

"Let's go find out," Stephanie said.

They hopped into Gallagher's Nissan, which was parked in front of *Just Jewelry*, and drove to *Chic Boutique*. They found Priscilla folding clothes. Another woman was busy with something behind the counter. It was still early, so there were no customers yet.

The woman called out to Priscilla that she was going out back for a little while.

"Can I help you find something?" Priscilla asked as the woman disappeared down a corridor and behind a door. It took Priscilla a few seconds to realize who they were. Her eyes flew open. "What are you doing here? I've already answered all your questions, and I spoke to the police like you wanted." She glanced over her shoulder nervously.

"Don't worry," Connie said. "We'll be discreet. We just want to know why you didn't go to the police on your own after you promised us you would."

Priscilla stared at the ground. "I was going to, but then I got scared. I was afraid I'd get in trouble."

"Get in trouble for what?" Gallagher asked. "For setting off the fire alarm, or for taking off without admitting that it was you?"

"Well, both. This hasn't been a good year for me, and you don't know my parents. I wanted to stay as far away from the police station as possible."

"Priscilla, we're talking about a murder investigation," Connie said. "And it's not a crime to accidentally set off a fire alarm."

"I know, it's just that I've already gotten into a lot of trouble this year. Some friends and I were caught shoplifting at one of the stores at the Coconut Point outdoor shopping mall in December. The owner of the store didn't press charges, but my parents were livid. Then, on New Year's Eve, my boyfriend and I got busted trying to use a fake ID to buy alcohol for a party. I didn't want to have to tell my parents that I messed up again. If they heard that I set off a fire alarm just before a man was killed, I'd be grounded for life. I was planning to go after we talked, but the more I thought about it, the more I figured I'd only get myself in more trouble."

"Priscilla, there is a murder investigation taking place, and the information you had could have helped the police track down the killer," Connie said. "It would have been helpful for the police to know sooner that the killer didn't set off the fire alarm as a diversion before poisoning Arnold. His family deserves justice."

"Not to mention that the sooner the police find the killer, the sooner Gallagher can reopen his restaurant and bring a lot of good people back to work," Stephanie added.

Priscilla let out a frustrated sigh. "I know. I know. You're right. I should have gone sooner. But in any case, I already talked to the police and told them exactly what happened. There's nothing more I can do."

The woman who had been out back while they talked returned to the sales floor. Priscilla looked nervously at her uninvited guests.

"Well, thank you for your assistance," Connie said, loudly enough for Priscilla's boss to hear. "You've been very helpful. We'll be sure to come back and buy something soon."

Chapter 13

CONNIE, GALLAGHER, AND STEPHANIE walked in silence from *Chic Boutique* back to Gallagher's car.

"If she were my daughter, I *would* ground her for life," Gallagher said, once they were out of earshot.

"I guess Zach was right. Priscilla wasn't covering up for murder. She was just trying to avoid getting into trouble with her parents," Connie said.

"Agreed. It sounds like her only crime was selfishness," Stephanie said.

"Now that we're fairly certain Priscilla isn't the killer, what do you think our next move should be?" Gallagher asked.

Connie reflected for a moment. "We know that Priscilla really was looking for the restroom and that

Fernando brought her there. On her way out, she accidentally set off the fire alarm, which gave the killer the opportunity to slip arsenic into Arnold's salad dressing."

"Unless Fernando had already poisoned Arnold's food in the kitchen," Stephanie said. "But if it *wasn't* Fernando, the deed had to be done during the chaos of the fire alarm. Dom, Ronnie, and Kendra were the only ones sitting at Arnold's table at that time, since Evan was outside on a phone call."

"We also know that there was rat poison, which contains arsenic, in the restaurant, so the killer could have either brought in the poison himself or herself or used the rat poison that was already in the restaurant," Stephanie said.

"According to Evan, Kendra had been following them around all week, so it is likely she was deliberately at the restaurant. She could have been looking for the right opportunity throughout her trip and the alarm provided it," Gallagher suggested.

"Have you found out who brought the rat poison into your restaurant?" Connie asked.

"No. I was planning to call all of my employees today, anyway, to see how they're doing and to reassure them that I'm doing everything I can to get us all back to work. I'll ask around about the rat poison."

"Perfect," Connie said. "Keep us posted on that."

"I wish we knew what Evan wanted to tell us yesterday," Gallagher said.

"Maybe we should talk to Ronnie and Dom again," Stephanie suggested. "I could drop in to express my concern for Evan. They *are* my neighbors, at least for two weeks out of the year."

"They weren't exactly friendly at the tennis match," Gallagher said. "They only talked to us because we had Evan's help. We no longer have that."

"We might as well give it a shot," Connie said. "We have nothing to lose. And while we're at it, we should also talk to Kendra again. We need to ask both her and Dom what they were talking about in the picture Gallagher obtained."

"Can you go now?" Gallagher asked.

"Why not? Now that I have Kelly, I feel a lot more comfortable being away from the shop. It's ironic. Part of the reason I brought on more help was so I could spend more time with Zach, but he keeps having to cancel our dates. The best laid plans…"

Gallagher started his car. "It's settled then. We're off to Stephanie's house to talk with Dom and Ronnie."

They parked at Stephanie's and walked over to the men's rental house. They heard some voices coming from the back of the house, so instead of ringing the doorbell, they ventured around to the lanai and found Ronnie and Dom having coffee.

Connie braced herself to receive a sarcastic greeting, as they had the last time.

"We thought we might see you sometime today," Dom said.

Ronnie gestured toward a few empty chairs. "Pull up a seat. I'm sure you have some questions for us."

Connie glanced at Gallagher and Stephanie. They seemed equally taken aback by the change in attitude.

"We didn't think you'd be all that happy to see us, judging from our last visit," Gallagher said.

"In our defense, you *did* suspect us of murdering our friend and colleague," Dom said.

"Fair enough."

"Although I'm sure we are still on the top of your suspect list," Ronnie said.

"So, why are you so willing to talk with us now?" Connie asked.

"I guess you could say we're both a little scared," Dom said. "We're willing to cooperate with anyone searching for Arnold's killer, since that person is probably the same one who kidnapped Evan. I guess we just have more at stake."

"What Dom means is that there's nothing we can do to help Arnold now, but we're very concerned about Evan. The faster the killer is found, the sooner we will be able to find Evan and get out of here," Ronnie said.

"We both refuse to go home without Evan. I already told my wife that I'm not leaving Sapphire Beach until this case is solved," Dom said.

"Evan left a note on my door sometime on Tuesday asking if we could meet on Wednesday," Stephanie said. "He said he had some information that he wanted to pass along to us. Did he mention anything about that to either of you?"

Ronnie shook his head. "I'm sure he would have told us if he had information."

Unless that information implicated Ronnie, Dom, or both of them.

"When was the last time you both saw Evan?" Connie asked.

"For me, it would have been about 3:00 on Tuesday afternoon," Dom said. "Evan, Ronnie, and I were catching some rays at the beach. Evan and Ronnie had had enough sun, so they went back to the rental. I stayed at the beach for another hour or so."

"Evan and I walked home together," Ronnie said. "Then he announced he was going for a walk. He left, and he never returned."

"Did he say anything else?" Stephanie asked.

"No. But before we went to the beach, he did meet with Kendra," Ronnie said.

"What time was that?" Connie asked.

"That would have been about 11:00 in the morning. Evan said he had to interview Kendra for an article he was working on and that he might as well take advantage of the fact that she was in town to get that done. They met at a coffee shop, but he was back by 1:00. That's when we all went to the beach."

Stephanie shivered, despite the sun beating down on them. "That means Evan left the note on my door either right after he returned from his meeting with Kendra or right before he disappeared."

"It appears that way," Ronnie said. "I'll bet Evan learned something incriminating about Kendra during his interview with her on Tuesday morning. Maybe he figured out that she was the killer and wanted to tell you."

"Why wouldn't he go straight to the police?" Connie asked.

Ronnie rubbed his chin. "Maybe he knew who the killer is, but needed your help proving it. Or maybe he wanted to run a theory by you to see what you thought."

"You could be right," Connie said.

Dom adamantly shook his head. "I find it too hard to believe that Kendra would have killed Arnold. And if she goes to jail, she won't get the magazine, anyway."

"She just might be cocky enough to think she could pull it off," Ronnie said.

"There is one more thing you should know," Dom added. "Evan mentioned to me on Tuesday night that he was trying to reach Fernando, but he wasn't able to find his address online, because he didn't know his last name."

"That's the night before Evan disappeared," Ronnie said. "You didn't tell me he said that."

"I just remembered as we were talking. I guess I'm not thinking clearly."

"Do you know what he wanted to talk to Fernando about?" Ronnie asked.

Dom shrugged. "He didn't say. He just said he remembered something and wanted to talk to Fernando about it."

"Stephanie, didn't Evan say he had a question for us in the note he left on your door?" Connie asked.

"He did. He said he had some information he wanted to share with us and a question he hoped we could answer for him. Maybe he was going to ask us for Fernando's address."

Gallagher looked skeptically at Dom.

"I just hope Evan is okay," Dom said. "We should have left Sapphire Beach last week. What were we thinking staying here with a killer on the loose?"

"We just have one more question for you," Connie said. "Dom, we'd like to ask you about a photo."

Gallagher opened the picture of Kendra whispering something to Dom shortly before Arnold died. "Another patron in the restaurant happened to snap this photo. Could you tell us what Kendra was saying to you here?"

Dom picked up his reading glasses from the table, put them on, and studied the photo on Gallagher's phone. "Oh, yes. Kendra was asking me if Arnold had changed his mind about selling the magazine. She knew that we were trying to convince him to sell while we were here on vacation. I told her that he still had no intention of selling." Dom's eyes widened. "You don't suppose that that was the moment Kendra decided to kill him, do you?"

"Don't go jumping to conclusions," Ronnie said. "It could have been the cook. Maybe Evan found his address after all and paid him a visit." Then he turned to Connie, Gallagher, and Stephanie. "We've told you everything we know. It's been a tough week for us. If you don't mind, I think you should probably leave."

"Of course," Gallagher said. "Please let us know if you think of anything else."

"What did you think?" Gallagher asked, once they had settled into the rockers on Stephanie's front porch. "Were they telling the truth?"

"Either one of them could be guilty," Stephanie said.

"Or they *both* could be. Maybe Evan figured out that they both killed Arnold together so they could sell the magazine," Connie said.

"Neither of them has a solid alibi for when Evan disappeared," Gallagher said. "They could definitely be covering for each other."

Connie stood up and opened Stephanie's front door. She grabbed the tennis racket, which was just inside, and practiced her backhand while they talked. It was easier to think when she was moving.

"Assuming the killer was either Ronnie or Dom, if Dom really did stay behind on the beach that day, Ronnie would have to have done it," Gallagher said. "Dom said he didn't leave the beach until an hour after Ronnie and Evan left, so it's conceivable that Ronnie could have killed him and then hid the body within that time frame, especially if he had it planned out."

"Unless Dom lied about staying on the beach," Connie said. She put the racket down and sat across from Gallagher. "When Dom was telling us about Evan wanting to talk to Fernando, you looked skeptical."

"Yeah, I don't trust Dom. I think he made that up."

"Why do you say that?" Connie asked.

"Well, Dom said Evan searched the Internet and couldn't find Fernando, because he didn't have his last name. Either Evan doesn't know how to do simple Internet research, or Dom is lying. All Evan would have to do is look at my website, and that's probably the first place he would have started. The website for my restaurant has a 'Meet the Staff' section. There's a picture of Fernando, along with his first and last name. It also says he's a resident of Sapphire Beach and how much he loves this town. Plus, Fernando is prominently featured on our social media sites and frequently tagged in various posts. If Evan were searching for Fernando's address, it wouldn't have taken him much time to find his address and probably his phone number, too."

"And Evan *is* a sports journalist, so I'd say it's a pretty safe bet he has some basic research skills," Connie pointed out. "You're right, Gallagher, that doesn't add up."

"I still say we can't rule out Kendra," Stephanie said. "If Ronnie and Dom were both telling the truth, and Evan really did go for a walk, Kendra could have found him and killed him."

"I'm not sure how plausible that is, since Evan is bigger and stronger than Kendra. But we should talk to her, anyway. She was one of the last people to see him before he disappeared," Connie said.

"And we need to ask her about the photo," Stephanie added.

Connie put Stephanie's tennis racket back inside the house. "I still have a couple of hours until I have to be back at the store. Let's go now."

Chapter 14

CONNIE, STEPHANIE, AND GALLAGHER drove to Palm Paradise in hopes of finding Kendra at home. They took the elevator to the sixth floor, and, for the second time this week, knocked on her door.

There was no answer.

"It's a beautiful day out. Maybe she's at the pool or the beach," Connie suggested. "Let's go up to my place and check."

They took the stairs up one floor to Connie's condo and stepped out on the balcony. Connie scanned the crowded pool area seven stories below. "She's not at the pool."

"I don't see her on the beach, either," Gallagher said, shielding his eyes from the sun with his hand. "I guess we'll have to come back later."

"Abby will be coming in at 4:00. How about if we try again after that? That will give me plenty of time to get back to the shop for my jewelry-making class tonight."

"Sounds like a plan," Gallagher said.

Gallagher and Stephanie drove Connie back to her shop, and, after a quick visit with Grace, they left.

Kelly and Grace stayed busy helping customers, while Connie continued her jewelry-making projects. When Grace's shift ended at 2:00, Connie put aside her tools and beads and assisted Kelly with the steady flow of customers.

The afternoon flew by, and before Connie knew it, Abby had arrived for her shift.

"Hey, Abby," Connie said when she walked through the door. Connie happened to glance at the time on a clock behind the circular checkout counter. "You're early."

At that moment, Connie noticed that Abby's complexion was unusually pale. Connie waited for the customer whose purchase she was ringing up to leave, then she took Abby to a corner. "Abby, are you okay? You don't look good."

She swallowed hard. "I think I just saw his face."

"The man who has been following you?" Connie asked.

Abby nodded.

Connie got Abby a water, then brought her to the oak table and pulled out a chair for her. "Tell me what happened."

"I arrived in town early for my shift this afternoon. I figured I'd grab a late lunch and a cup of coffee and enjoy the sunshine. I got my food and was eating it on a bench by the pier when I got that feeling again."

"Like someone was following you?" Connie asked.

"Uh-huh. I turned around suddenly and made eye contact with a man who had been staring at me. He got a panicked look on his face. He turned around abruptly and bolted in the other direction."

"What did he look like?" Connie asked.

"I would say he was in his early thirties, I guess. He had light hair. But what I remember most was his expression. He definitely didn't want me to see him. I stood to go talk to him, but he was gone before I could even stand up."

"Are you sure you've never seen him before?" Connie asked.

"Positive. I have no idea who he was."

Connie leaned forward and rested her arms on the table. "This can't go on. We need to figure out who this guy is, or you'll be living in fear."

"I agree, but what am I supposed to do?"

"Let's think about it tonight while we work," Connie said. "I have to do something with Gallagher and Stephanie, but I'll be back in time for tonight's class. After that, we can regroup and try to come up with a plan to handle this situation. We'll think of something."

Abby breathed a sigh of relief. "Okay. Thanks."

Stephanie and Gallagher arrived right on schedule. While they were stuck in the boulevard traffic that came with the tourist season, they caught Connie up on their busy afternoon.

"I know how the rat poison got into my restaurant," Gallagher said. "I spent the afternoon calling all my employees to reassure them that we are doing everything we can to get the restaurant reopened. I also asked everyone about the rat poison. It turns out my hostess brought in a package on one of my days off. Apparently, she saw a rat scurrying away while she was accompanying some patrons to their table. She said the customers didn't see it, but it freaked her out. So, before her next shift, she bought a bag of rat poison. She said that's what her parents used to use at home. She put some of it in one of the corners of the dining room and left the bag with its remaining contents in the storage room. She had been meaning to tell me, but she kept forgetting."

"Oh, my goodness," Connie said. "She had no idea that you shouldn't use rat poison in a restaurant?"

"No. She felt awful. She was terrified that she contributed to Arnold's death. It took me a while to calm her down and to convince her that it's more likely that the killer brought in their own poison. I called Zach, though, to let him know."

"That means it's still possible that the killer is Fernando," Connie said. "He could have seen the rat poison in the storage room and used it to poison Arnold's salad dressing."

"It's possible," Gallagher said. "But after we dropped you off, we spun by Fernando's house. He said that Evan never contacted him."

"Do you believe him?"

"Connie, we stopped by without giving him any advanced notice, because we wanted to see his honest reaction," Gallagher said. "I was looking directly into his eyes. I truly believe he was telling the truth."

"I do, too," Stephanie said.

When they finally arrived at Palm Paradise, Gallagher parked in Connie's outdoor parking space. On their way upstairs they saw Jessica, the condo management employee whose office was located off the building's lush lobby.

"Gallagher!" Jessica said. "It's so good to see you again."

They had gotten to know one another when everyone was stuck at Palm Paradise during Hurricane Emery in August. "I was so sorry to hear what happened in your restaurant last week. How are you doing?"

"I'm hanging in there," Gallagher said. "I'm anxious to reopen, though."

"I can imagine. Let me guess," Jessica added with a smirk. "The three of you are back at it, trying to solve this case."

"You guessed it," Gallagher said.

"One of our suspects is renting a condo in Palm Paradise," Connie said. "But you didn't hear that from us."

Jessica's jaw fell. "Not Kendra."

Now it was Connie's turn to be surprised. "How did you know that? Of all the renters in the building, why would you think of Kendra?"

"Well, I saw on the news this morning that Evan was missing. And I know they have an, um, relationship," Jessica said.

"Wait, *what*?" Connie asked. "You mean a *romantic* relationship?"

"Oops," Jessica said. "I guess that wasn't common knowledge. It's just, you know, I can see the lobby from my office, and he visits her frequently. I've seen her walk him to the door several times, and it's definitely not a platonic relationship."

Jessica laughed at the trio, who were still looking at her with their mouths open. "Judging from your expressions, I'd say that was news to you. I didn't realize it was a secret."

"I'm guessing it is, since his bosses didn't seem to know anything about it, either," Connie said. "Do you know how serious they were?"

Jessica waited for a couple to pass by before she answered. "I'm not saying this to gossip. I'm just telling you, because it might be relevant to your case. They couldn't have been very serious. Kendra stays here every time she comes to Sapphire Beach, and she is usually seeing a different guy every time." Jessica said. "Come to think of it, Evan hasn't been here since Arnold died."

"That's interesting," Connie said. "Evan pretty much sold her out as a possible suspect. She wants to purchase the magazine that the victim co-owned with two colleagues. Maybe Evan suspected Kendra of murdering one of his bosses and broke it off with her."

"Our list of questions for Kendra is growing," Connie said.

"You should be able to talk with her now. I just saw her come in a few minutes ago," Jessica said.

"Thanks for the information," Gallagher said as they headed toward the elevator.

"Glad I could help," Jessica yelled after them. "Good luck."

They took the elevator to the sixth floor. As they approached Kendra's door, Connie could hear the television. "She's definitely in there."

Gallagher knocked four times.

When Kendra opened the door, she didn't seem surprised to see them. "I heard what happened to Evan. I figured the three of you would be by asking more questions. Come on in. I only have a few minutes. I have a date tonight."

She apparently got over Evan pretty quickly.

"Let's cut to the chase. I'm sure you're here to ask me if I know what happened to Evan. I'm afraid I won't be much help. I have no idea. His disappearance was as much of a shock to me as anyone else."

Connie decided to come at it from another angle. "We know about you and Evan. I live in Palm Paradise. I've heard the rumors," she said, exaggerating the facts. "If you don't mind my saying, you don't even seem a little upset that a man you are dating is missing."

Kendra motioned for them to follow her to the dining room table. After they sat down, she leaned back in her chair. "Don't get me wrong. Evan was a lot of fun. But it was never serious between us. We had a good time together when we would run into each other on trips. But that was it. Besides, after Arnold died, he pretty much ignored me. I think he actually suspected me of killing Arnold. That kind of squashed any attraction I had to him."

"I guess it would," Stephanie said.

"So, you have no idea what could have happened to him?" Connie asked.

"All I know is what I heard. Evan went for a walk yesterday afternoon and never came back. I mean, think about it. Do you think I could abduct a grown, athletic man while he was walking down the street? Sure, I'm in decent shape, but you overestimate my physical capabilities."

Kendra did have a point. It was one thing to slip poison into someone's food. But it would be quite another to either kill or kidnap a guy in broad daylight.

"We heard you were together on Tuesday afternoon before Evan disappeared," Connie said.

"You mean during the interview?"

Connie nodded.

"He interviewed me for a feature article. It was all business. He didn't even come here. He insisted we meet in a public place." Kendra shook her head. "I think the guy was actually afraid of being alone with me."

Connie couldn't blame Evan. Kendra *was* a suspect in his friend's murder.

"I still say you should concentrate your efforts on Ronnie and Dom. Trust me when I say that they were very eager to sell *Tennis Times,* and Arnold was the only holdout."

Gallagher took his phone from his pocket. "This photo was taken by someone in my restaurant shortly before Arnold was killed. Could you tell me what you were saying to Dom?"

Kendra took Gallagher's phone and examined the photo. "Oh, *that*? As I told you the last time we talked, I'm a persistent woman. I was asking him if Arnold showed any sign of agreeing to sell."

"And had he?" Gallagher asked.

"Not even a little."

Chapter 15

AFTER THEY FINISHED talking with Kendra, Gallagher and Stephanie brought Connie back to *Just Jewelry*.

"Kendra's attitude really bothered me," Stephanie said as they were driving down the boulevard. "She was so nonchalant about the fact that her former beau is missing. He could even be dead! I feel like we're more worried about Evan than she is."

"Her carelessness *is* disconcerting," Connie said. "But then again, she said Evan accused her of murder. Maybe she's just hardened."

"Or maybe Kendra was just using Evan to try to persuade Arnold to sell the magazine," Gallagher suggested. "Just because she uses people doesn't make her a killer. My money is on Dom. I'm convinced he was lying about Fernando. Ronnie said he left Dom behind at the beach when Evan disappeared, but that doesn't mean Dom stayed there."

"If we rule out Kendra, that leaves Dom, Ronnie, and, unfortunately, Fernando," Connie said. "But before we decide on our next move, I need to shift gears." She filled Gallagher and Stephanie in on what was happening with Abby.

"Wow, that's intense!" Gallagher said. "What is she going to do?"

"I don't know, but I have to help her think of something. She won't tell the police, because she's afraid it's all in her imagination and doesn't think there's much they could do, anyway. But she hasn't been herself for nearly two weeks. I'm worried about her."

"Let me help you," Gallagher said. "You and Abby shouldn't try to handle this alone."

Stephanie nodded her agreement. "That's not a bad idea. If this man is crazy, maybe he'd be less likely to try something if there's another guy around."

"I think Abby would be open to that. Why don't I have Abby call me the next time she feels as though she's being followed? Then we could keep an eye on her at a distance and see if we can't get to the bottom of what's going on."

"I'm bummed," Stephanie said. "I want to be part of the stakeout, too."

"You can be," Connie said. "You can hang tight at home, and if something goes wrong, we'll let you know, and you can call the police."

Gallagher and Stephanie came into the shop with Connie, and the three of them proposed their plan to Abby.

"I really appreciate this, you guys. I was planning to come downtown at noon tomorrow to do some errands and have lunch before my shift. It's supposed to be a beautiful day, so I thought I'd take advantage. I'll text you if anything doesn't feel right."

"That's perfect," Connie said. "Both Kelly and Grace will be working, so I'll be able to leave the shop at a moment's notice."

"And I'll be nearby, as well," Gallagher said.

Gallagher and Stephanie left as students began arriving for Connie's jewelry-making class. Since it was the high season in Sapphire Beach, it was a larger-than-normal class, with several beginners trying out Connie's class for the first time. They kept Connie and Abby busy all evening answering questions and demonstrating basic techniques.

"Are you sure you want to follow through with our plan tomorrow?" Abby asked Connie once the class was over and everyone had left. "I don't want to put you and Gallagher in any danger."

"I'm positive. We need to get to the bottom of whatever is happening."

"I'll be so embarrassed if it's all in my imagination."

"I'll be relieved if it is," Connie said. "There's no reason for you to be embarrassed. You should always trust your instincts. And don't worry about Gallagher. It's good for him to have something to take his mind off his own problems. Besides, if someone *is* following you, they're not likely to try anything funny in broad daylight."

As the words came out of Connie's mouth, she thought of Evan disappearing in the middle of the afternoon, and her confidence waned. She didn't mention that insight to Abby.

"I suppose you're right," Abby said.

"Would you like me to follow you home tonight?" Connie asked.

Abby shook her head. "No. But let's walk to our cars together, just to be safe."

Connie fastened Ginger's leash, and the two walked together to the parking lot at the end of their street. Connie glanced at *Gallagher's Tropical Shack* after locking her door. The sounds of laughter and clinking dishes that normally drifted across the street were replaced with silence.

Connie and Abby instinctively sped up as they made their way to their cars.

After Connie and Ginger walked Abby to her car, they got into Connie's Jetta. She waited for Abby to pull away before putting her vehicle into drive and returning home.

On Friday morning, both Kelly and Grace were already in the store when Connie arrived. Connie explained to her coworkers their plan to help Abby.

"I'm glad you and Gallagher are going to help her," Kelly said. "I haven't known Abby for long, but it's obvious that she hasn't been herself lately."

What began as a slow morning suddenly turned busy. As the noon hour approached, Connie let Kelly and Grace handle the customers so that she would be free to leave at a moment's notice if Abby should call.

Just before noon, Gallagher texted Connie to let her know that he was already downtown standing by in a coffee shop, and Stephanie was waiting by her phone at home in case anything went wrong. Abby also texted to say she was on her way downtown.

While Connie waited, she worked on a seafoam green-beaded bracelet to match a necklace she had finished the previous week. As her fingers strung beads onto the wire, her thoughts drifted to her plans with Zach the following evening. Since it was Take Three of their anniversary date, she already knew what she was going to wear. She said a quick prayer that nothing would interfere with their evening this time around.

As noon turned into 1:00, Connie began to lose hope that Abby would run into her mystery stalker.

Until quarter past one, when she received a text from Abby.

I'm by the pier, and I think he's following me.

Connie forwarded Abby's text to Gallagher, informed Kelly and Grace that she was leaving, and quickly headed for the pier.

When she arrived, Connie spotted Abby sitting on a blanket in the sand, not too far from the weather-beaten wooden pier that was an iconic image of Sapphire Beach. Connie walked discreetly past Abby and nodded so Abby would feel safe, then looped back to a bench just off the beach, where she had an unobstructed view of Abby and her surroundings. When she sat down, she noticed Gallagher standing behind one of the wood pilings beneath the pier, also surveying the scene.

Connie texted Abby. *Do you see him?*

Abby looked around, then sent Connie a message. *Not right now. But I see Gallagher. You guys are the best.*

They waited for what seemed like an eternity, but, in reality, was probably only ten minutes, until a man who matched Abby's description of her stalker emerged from behind a nearby restaurant and slowly walked toward Abby.

Abby looked up and froze. Then she reached for her phone and texted Connie. *That's him. The guy coming towards me is the same guy I saw the other day. I think he's the one who has been following me.*

Connie forced herself to wait until he was a little closer to Abby, so he couldn't run away. Then she waved at Gallagher and pointed at the guy, who was approaching a frozen Abby. Connie jogged toward Abby, and Gallagher shot out from behind the pier. They both reached her at the same time and surrounded the man, who was now only five feet away from Abby's blanket.

The man stopped in his tracks when he saw Connie and Gallagher, and the color drained from his face.

Gallagher circled behind the man and firmly grasped his shoulder while Connie sat next to Abby on the blanket.

"I don't know who you are," Gallagher said. "But you have some explaining to do."

He shook Gallagher's hand from his shoulder and crouched down in the sand. The man looked as if he were about to cry. He stared at Abby as if she were the only person in the world. "Are you Abby?" he asked. "Abby Burns?"

"Before I answer that question, I want to know who *you* are, and why you're following me." There was a note of panic in her voice.

The mystery man sat down cross-legged in front of Abby and stared at her a little longer, seemingly unable to speak. Then his gaze softened. "I didn't mean to scare you. My name is Wesley Davidson, but you can call me Wes. I think I'm your brother."

Chapter 16

"MY *BROTHER*?" Abby asked. She shook her head. "That's impossible. I only have one sibling. I'm positive that I don't have a brother. I'm afraid you must be mistaken."

Gallagher sat on the blanket on the other side of Abby, so that he and Connie formed a protective wall around their young friend.

"I'm sorry that you wasted your time," Abby said.

Wes shook his head, never taking his eyes off Abby. "I don't think I did. Your parents are Francine and Doug Burns, who were high school sweethearts. And you have a younger sister named Sophia."

"That's right, but..." Abby's voice trailed off.

"Your parents, my biological parents, gave me up for adoption when I was a baby. They had me when they were in high school, thirty-three years ago."

Abby studied Wes. "My parents *did* date in high school. Then they went to separate colleges and didn't see each other again until they graduated." Abby looked at Connie. "My parents reconnected at a high school reunion and got married soon after. But they never told my sister or me anything about a child they gave up for adoption. Why would they hide that from us?"

Connie examined Wes's features. He had the same light brown hair and round brown eyes as Abby. It certainly was possible. Wes's voice was brimming with emotion as he spoke. What reason could he possibly have to lie?

Abby was apparently thinking the same thing. She smiled at Wes. "I can see the resemblance for sure."

She looked at Connie, who nodded. "I can, too."

"I need to talk to my parents and my sister," Abby said.

"I know it's a lot to spring on you," Wes said.

"Why didn't you just approach Abby, rather than follow her around all week?" Gallagher asked. "You scared her."

"I'm sorry. I had to be in the area for a conference, so I extended my stay to come to Sapphire Beach. At first, I just wanted to see you, Abby, but then I determined that I would introduce myself. I kept losing my nerve. I didn't know how you'd react. I know from social media that you are a graduate student at Florida Sands University and that your sister is a junior at Colorado State. I did some research after my adoptive parents passed away in a car accident two years ago." Wes pulled out his wallet and showed Abby a photo of him with his parents.

"I'm so sorry, Wes," Abby said.

"My adoption was an open one, but I never reached out. I guess I didn't feel the need while my parents were alive. When my folks passed away, I became increasingly more curious. I finally looked at the records last year. That's when I searched for my parents on social media and found out about you and Sophia. I don't have any siblings, so I was thrilled to learn about the two of you. The last thing I wanted to do was to scare you."

Wes took out his wallet and handed his driver's license to Gallagher. "See, I'm not lying. If I were a crazy person, would I show you my ID?"

Abby stared at Wes. "So, there's no doubt? You saw the records and you know for sure we are siblings?"

Wes smiled and nodded. "We definitely have the same parents, so that makes us brother and sister."

Suddenly, the shock seemed to wear off and Abby threw herself into Wes's arms. He was still squatting in the sand, and Abby nearly knocked him backwards. "In that case, it's wonderful to meet you, Wes. I can't wait to introduce you to Sophia. Tell me everything about yourself."

Wes laughed as a tear streamed down his face.

"We'll leave you two to get acquainted," Connie said, glancing at Gallagher, who was wearing a smile as broad as Connie's own.

"I'll see you tonight, Connie," Abby said.

"Wes, you're welcome to hang out at the shop tonight," Connie offered. "I'd be happy to let Abby go a little early so you can continue your conversation."

He smiled a familiar smile - familiar because it resembled Abby's. "Thank you, Connie. I might take you up on that. I'm only here for a few more days, so I'd like to make the most of them."

Connie and Gallagher left the siblings to get acquainted and walked back to *Just Jewelry*.

"All's well that ends well," Gallagher said. "That couldn't have been a more perfect ending. It was a nice diversion from what's going on in my own life."

"Speaking of which, it's after lunchtime. Let's tell Stephanie to meet us downtown so we can decide over lunch what our next step should be with the investigation. After what just happened with Wes and Abby, I feel like we're on a mystery-solving roll."

"I hope so," Gallagher said. "Tonight will mark one week since my restaurant has been closed, and my bank account can't take much more of this. I talked to Zach yesterday, and he said to plan on losing at least a couple more week's revenue. I'm trying to remain optimistic, but it's getting increasingly difficult."

Connie put an encouraging hand on Gallagher's shoulder. "We're going to figure this out, my friend. I'm going to make it a priority until you're reopened. You'll see. In the grand scheme of things, this will only be a minor setback."

He smiled gratefully. "I hope so."

Just then, Gallagher's phone rang. "Speaking of Stephanie..."

"She's probably wondering how things went with Abby. Tell her to meet us at *Smitty's Sandwich Shop* so we can fill her in and regroup."

Gallagher nodded as he accepted the call, but Stephanie did most of the talking.

"Abby's okay," Gallagher said. "We'll fill you in when we see you... Okay, I'll be right there. I'll see if Connie can come too," he said, disconnecting the call.

"What's up?" Connie asked.

"Stephanie thinks Dom's wife is in town and staying at their rental. She saw the two of them a few minutes ago walking toward the beach holding hands with lounge chairs and towels. She wants to try to talk to his wife, but she doesn't want to do it alone. I'm going there now."

"Shoot. If I go, I won't make it back before Grace leaves. I'm sure they'll be at the beach for a while. Let's quickly stop by *Just Jewelry* so I can make sure Kelly is okay with being alone for a little while. If not, you can go and fill me in after."

Chapter 17

CONNIE AND GALLAGHER quickly shifted directions from *Smitty's Sandwich Shop* to *Just Jewelry.*

"How did it go with Abby?" Grace eagerly asked when they walked in the store.

"It turns out Abby's stalker is the brother she never knew she had. It's a long story with a happy ending. We'll let Abby fill you in on the details, but for now, we need to get to the beach to talk to someone about the case. Kelly, would you be okay alone in the store for about an hour?"

"I'll stay with Kelly until you get back," Grace insisted. "It's been pretty busy. Plus, I want to learn more about Abby's brother, so I think I'll stay until she gets here, anyway. Besides, I feel better knowing the two of you are with Stephanie, so you're the ones doing me a favor. I know this case is important to her, but I don't want her putting herself in danger to help solve it."

"I won't let that happen," Gallagher said. "If I feel as though her safety could be in jeopardy, I'll insist that she move in with you until this case is solved."

"I won't let that happen," Gallagher said. "If I feel as though her safety could be in jeopardy, I'll insist that she move in with you until this case is solved."

"Thank you, Gallagher. I know I can count on you."

"It's settled then. We're off to the beach," he said.

They drove Connie's Jetta down Sapphire Beach Boulevard and turned onto Stephanie's street. When they arrived at her house, she was waiting for them on the front porch.

"I saw Dom heading back to the house, so I think his wife is alone," Stephanie said.

"That's even better. We might be able to glean more information if we can talk to her by herself," Connie said.

They speed-walked down Stephanie's street, crossed the boulevard, and took the public access alley to the beach. Stephanie scanned the area, then pointed to an attractive woman with auburn hair and an athletic build lying on a lounge chair. "That's her."

They took off their shoes before stepping onto the warm, dry sand and stopped in front of the woman's lounge chair. Since they were blocking her sun, she opened her eyes and gave them a puzzled look.

"Can I help you?"

"Good afternoon, ma'am. My name is Gallagher McKeon, and I own the restaurant where Arnold passed away last Friday. Would you mind if we talked to you for a few minutes?"

She sat up and put on a navy-blue sun visor, which matched her navy and white bathing suit. "I suppose so. Dom and Ronnie mentioned that the restaurant owner and his friends have been investigating. But I only know what Dom and Ronnie told me. I was home in northern California at the time of Arnold's passing. When I heard what happened to Evan, and when Dom informed me that he wasn't coming home until this case was solved, I decided to fly out here. I'm Judy, by the way."

Connie sat on the sand facing Judy, and Gallagher and Stephanie followed suit. "I'm Connie, and this is Stephanie. You met Gallagher."

Judy nodded politely.

"Do you have any idea who could have done this to Arnold?" Connie asked.

"Dom, Ronnie, and I were talking about that all night. Ronnie thinks it might have been Kendra, and Dom said something about one of the cooks in the restaurant having had a grudge against Arnold."

"You mean Fernando," Connie said.

"Yes, he's the one. Honestly, I can't imagine Kendra doing something like that." Judy paused. "I imagine that Dom and Ronnie are prime suspects in your minds."

They remained silent. Connie was trying to think of a diplomatic way to tell this woman that her husband was her prime suspect.

But before Connie could say anything, Judy continued. "I would probably think the same thing if I were in your shoes. Dom and Ronnie very much wanted to sell the magazine, and Arnold was the only one holding out. My husband and I have both worked hard our whole lives. We just want to retire early and enjoy the finer things in life." Judy gestured to the crystal blue water and white silky sand that surrounded them. "But, my goodness, neither Dom or Ronnie would ever have killed for that reason."

"From what we learned," Gallagher said, "your husband had more to gain from Arnold's death than an early retirement."

Judy knit her brow. "I don't follow you."

"We know about his gambling debt," Connie said.

"I'm afraid you're mistaken. My husband doesn't have any gambling debt."

Connie, Gallagher, and Stephanie exchanged a puzzled glance.

"I'm the numbers gal in our family. I handle all the finances. Dom turns his paycheck over to me every week. I would absolutely know if he were gambling. If somebody told you that, they either made a big mistake or were lying. I don't like to gossip, but if anyone has a gambling debt, it's likely Ronnie. He's a big fan of casinos. He's always trying to convince Dom to go on gambling trips, but we both get bored easily at casinos."

Connie studied Judy while she spoke. She could be covering for her husband.

"One last question," Connie said. "What about Evan? If you had to venture a guess, what do you think happened to him?"

Judy readjusted her visor. "It's a mystery to me. Dom thinks Evan might have discovered something critical about the case. He suspects that whoever killed Arnold knew that and made sure that he disappeared. All I know for sure is that I've never seen Dom so upset."

"But Dom has no idea who that could be?" Gallagher asked.

"I think you know as much as I do about what Dom thinks. It seems that Evan was trying to track down Fernando, because he wanted to ask him about something he discovered. Maybe Evan confronted him, and it didn't go well. Dom said that Arnold really made a fool of him at his previous place of employment." Judy hesitated, then continued. "Arnold really had a way of humiliating people. He was a phenomenal tennis player, but he also had a real arrogant streak. He brought a lot to the magazine in terms of credibility and notoriety. But it's been a struggle dealing with his ego over the years."

"So, why did they all go on vacation together so often?"

"The first year, Ronnie and Dom tried to go without him, but Arnold loved traveling. Ultimately, they just couldn't shake him. He sort of came with the package, so they made the best of it. But they never would have harmed him or Evan. You should focus your attention on Kendra and Fernando. It had to be one of them."

"They are on our list of suspects," Connie assured her.

"Kendra wanted that magazine something fierce. She floundered for a while after her tennis career ended, and this magazine was her hope of regaining the respect of her peers. I can't say for sure, but I suspect she even got involved with Evan in hopes that he could persuade Arnold to sell it. Of course, Evan didn't have that type of influence over Arnold."

Connie nodded. "We heard that they were involved. We'll keep that in mind."

It seemed they had gotten all the information from Judy that they were going to get, so they thanked her for her time and left.

"What do you guys think?" Stephanie asked, as they walked back.

"I find it strange that she agreed to talk with us so easily," Connie said. "I was prepared to work hard to get her to share her thoughts with us. It was almost too easy. She doesn't even know us."

"Maybe she genuinely believes her husband is innocent and figured it couldn't do any harm," Stephanie suggested.

"Or she might have been so cooperative, because she wanted to throw suspicion off her husband," Connie said. "She denied that Dom has any gambling debt, but Evan, Kendra, and Ronnie all told us that he did. If she's telling the truth about handling the finances in their family, she either knows about his debt and is covering for him, or Dom was getting his gambling money somewhere besides his weekly paycheck."

"Dom could be playing his wife," Gallagher said. "She could be completely in the dark about everything."

Stephanie sighed. "So, I guess we didn't learn much from that conversation. We don't know if she was lying or in the dark about Dom's gambling. I'm sorry I asked you both to rush over."

"Don't be silly. I'm glad you called us," Connie said, as they arrived back at Stephanie's. "Every conversation brings us a step closer to finding the killer. But I really should be getting back to the shop. Grace is covering for me. Do you want a ride back, Gallagher?"

"That's okay. Stephanie can take me back later to get my car. I want to fill her in on what happened with Abby."

"Don't forget to eat lunch. We skipped it, remember?"

Gallagher rubbed his stomach and groaned. "How could I forget?"

"Connie, let me make you a sandwich so you don't have to stop on your way back. I made some chicken salad earlier, and I have plenty left. You can take it with you," Stephanie said.

"Thanks. That sounds great."

Connie and Gallagher followed Stephanie inside the house and into her kitchen. When Stephanie entered the room, she stopped abruptly, causing Connie to nearly plow into her.

"What are you doing?" Connie asked.

Stephanie turned around wide-eyed, then stared at the kitchen table.

Connie and Gallagher stepped around Stephanie so they could see what she was looking at.

There was no missing the large bowl of wilted salad, which had been placed in the middle of Stephanie's kitchen table, with a tented note that read, "Enjoy."

"Did you make that salad?" Connie asked.

Stephanie shook her head. "That was not here when we left for the beach. Someone came into my house and put it there while we were talking to Judy. Besides, why would I make a wilted salad? I don't even have lettuce in my house right now."

"Are you sure?" Gallagher asked. "Maybe it was there but you just didn't go into the kitchen."

"I'm positive. I came in here to get some water just before you guys arrived. It wasn't here."

"Was the door locked while we were gone?" Connie asked.

Stephanie shook her head. "No. This is a safe neighborhood, and we're far from the downtown area. I don't lock the door unless I'm leaving for the day."

Connie pulled her phone from her pocket. "Don't touch anything. I'm calling Zach."

Chapter 18

ZACH ARRIVED AT STEPHANIE'S house within ten minutes. He sent the salad in question to be analyzed, and he sat with Connie, Stephanie, and Gallagher in the living room while they recounted what happened.

"I examined every room in the house after Connie called you, and nothing was out of place," Stephanie informed Zach. "As far as I can tell, whoever did this walked through the front door, put the salad and note on the table, and left. The person had to have made the salad before entering my house, because the food wasn't from my kitchen."

"There weren't any fingerprints, either," Zach said. "The perpetrator probably wore gloves. I'll talk to your neighbors and see if anybody saw anything."

Gallagher took Stephanie's hand. "I think you should crash at your mother's place for the time being. I don't like the idea of you being here alone. And besides, I gave Grace my word that if I felt you could be in danger, then I would insist that you stay with her."

"Gallagher's right," Zach said. "There's no point taking any unnecessary chances. Somebody was clearly trying to send you a message, and we don't know how far they will go to drive that message home."

Stephanie didn't give them a hard time. "Okay. When Gallagher leaves, I'll pack some things and head over to my mother's."

"Speaking of Grace, I need to get back to the shop," Connie said. "She's covering for me."

Connie made a quick stop on her way back to the store to grab that sandwich she never got from Stephanie and took it back to *Just Jewelry*. While she was eating, she caught Kelly and Grace up on their conversation with Judy and the wilted salad that was planted on Stephanie's table.

"I'm glad Gallagher convinced Stephanie to stay with me, but I don't like this one bit. Somebody better solve this case quickly, because Stephanie will want to return home eventually."

"She said she'd be over a little later," Connie said.

Grace grabbed her purse from behind the counter. "I was going to wait for Abby before leaving, but I think I'll go home and cook dinner, in case Stephanie is hungry when she comes over. Hopefully, Gallagher will come, too. Tell Abby I'm excited to hear about her brother, but I'll have to catch up with her tomorrow."

"Will do." Connie said.

At 4:00 on the nose, Abby and Wes bounded into the store laughing and chatting away.

"How are you two?" Connie asked. But judging from their wide grins, they were relishing getting to know each other.

"We are great," Abby said. "I can't believe I was afraid of Wes! He's the sweetest big brother ever."

"Have you called your parents yet?" Connie asked.

"Not yet. We'll do that later. For now, we're just learning about each other. Wes is a mortgage broker. He is married to the super-cool Leah Davidson, my sister-in-law."

Abby tapped a few times on her phone. "Wes forwarded me these pictures of my niece, Charlotte. Can you believe I have a niece? She is six and loves to write, just like her Auntie Abby. I can't wait to meet her and her mom. And can you believe they only live a couple of hours away from my parents' home in Colorado? I can't wait for everyone to meet. They are going to love Wes."

At that, Wes's smile somehow managed to grow even broader.

"You guys have to spend Christmas with us next year, since you live so close. I'll bet my parents are going to insist. They are going to spoil Charlotte. So, are Sophia and I, for that matter."

Connie couldn't help but smile as Abby barely took a breath between sentences. "I'm so happy for you two. Wes, you're welcome to hang out here tonight. Evenings are usually pretty slow."

"I appreciate the offer, but I'm going back to my rental. I want to call Leah and fill her in on my day. Abby and I are going to meet up for breakfast tomorrow and decide how to best tell her, I mean *our*, parents."

"Wonderful," Connie said. "I hope to see you again soon. And this time, I promise not to almost tackle you."

Shortly after Wes left, foot traffic began to slow down. Abby talked nonstop about Wes, Leah, and Charlotte. After the past week that Abby spent believing someone might be stalking her, it was refreshing to see her giddy with excitement.

While Abby was helping a customer, Gallagher and Stephanie popped in.

"Your mother went home to cook dinner in case you guys get hungry," Connie said.

"That's sweet, but I think I lost my appetite," Gallagher said. "This whole situation went from bad to worse today. Zach called Stephanie while we were on our way here with some puzzling news."

"What did he say?" Connie asked.

"He said that both Dom and Ronnie have alibis for the whole salad incident. They were having drinks with a neighbor."

Connie paused to let the news sink in. "Whoever left the salad *had* to have been the killer. This doesn't make sense." She sat down at the table to think. "Maybe Kendra or Fernando are guilty, after all."

"That's what we were thinking, too," Gallagher said. "That puts Fernando at the top of our suspect list again. I'm doing my best not to let this news get me down, but it's a struggle."

"I'm so sorry," Abby said.

"By the way, Abby, Gallagher told me about what happened earlier today with your brother," Stephanie said.

"Can you believe it? I feel like I'm walking on air. I have a brother, sister-in-law, and niece I never knew about."

Stephanie gave Abby a hug. "That was the reason we were coming here in the first place. I wanted to congratulate you. I'm thrilled that your story has such a happy ending."

"Are you headed to Grace's now?" Connie asked.

"Eventually," Stephanie said. "Gallagher wants to talk to Fernando one more time."

"I want to ask him where he was earlier today during the salad incident. Also, it's no secret that Fernando used to gamble too much. He once told me that he spent a lot of time in the casino at Immokalee. Maybe he remembers seeing Dom there. It's a long shot, but it would be helpful to confirm that Dom really is the one with the gambling problem," Gallagher said.

"Isn't that irrelevant at this point?" Stephanie asked. "Dom and Ronnie have an alibi for today."

"Not necessarily," Connie said. "If one of them is working with Kendra, she could have left the salad. Our conversation with Judy hasn't been sitting well with me, either. It can't hurt to see what Fernando knows."

"Does that mean you're coming with us?" Stephanie asked.

Connie looked over at Abby.

"Go!" Abby said. "Who am I to stand in the way of justice?"

"Thanks, Abby. I won't be long," Connie said.

Ten minutes later, Connie, Gallagher, and Stephanie were sitting in Fernando's home on the other side of town. He was cooking spaghetti when they arrived, and the smell of gravy filled his tiny trailer.

"It smells amazing in here," Stephanie said, closing her eyes and inhaling the scent.

"Thanks. It's my top secret marinara sauce. I like to make a big batch and freeze it. After cooking all day for others, I'm not always in the mood to cook for myself at the end of a shift. Speaking of working, any news of when we can reopen?" Fernando asked.

"Unfortunately, no. We are doing our best, but we haven't found the killer yet. That's actually why we came by."

"Could you tell us where you were today between 1:30 and 2:00?" Connie asked.

Fernando picked up a wooden spoon and stirred the contents of a large stainless steel pot. "Sure. I was in the waiting room at my mechanic's place, waiting for them to replace a tire. They were really busy, so I brought the car in at 1:00 and didn't leave until 2:30."

"And you were in the waiting room the whole time?" Connie asked.

"Yeah, I just sat there reading magazines."

Gallagher breathed a sigh of relief. "That's great news."

"That I busted my tire?" Fernando asked, slightly annoyed. "It wasn't great news when it happened. It was the last thing I needed now that I'm out of work."

Connie didn't give Gallagher a chance to explain why it was, indeed, good news. "Fernando, the last time we talked to you, you mentioned that you try to stay out of the casinos, because you..." Connie hesitated, wondering how to put it delicately.

"Because I've been known to gamble away my paycheck," Fernando supplied.

"Well," Connie continued, "we were wondering if you have any friends who still frequent the casinos."

"For sure," Fernando said. "Why do you ask?"

"Well, we were told by a few people that Dom, one of the guys at Arnold's table the night he died, was a heavy gambler. We were wondering if you could ask around to confirm whether or not it's true."

"I don't have to ask any of my friends about that. He definitely was. I would see him in the casino at Immokalee whenever they were in town. Because of what a jerk Arnold was to me, I avoided him when I saw him, but he would always be there whenever they were in town. Fortunately, he was usually alone. If Arnold had been there, I probably would have left."

"And you're *sure* it was Dom?" Connie asked.

"I guess. I don't know the guy's name. He was the one with brown hair sitting to Arnold's left."

Connie thought for a moment, trying to remember where Dom was seated the night

Arnold died. "I think Dom was on Arnold's right. He has dark brown hair and was wearing a black collared shirt with short sleeves."

"No, the guy I've seen in the casino has light brown hair. He was wearing a printed shirt last Friday night."

Connie's heart nearly skipped a beat.

"That's *Ronnie*!" Stephanie said.

"But that doesn't make sense. Why would Ronnie, Evan, and Kendra *all* say that Dom was the one with the gambling problem?" Gallagher asked.

"Thank you for your time," Connie said to Fernando. "You've been super helpful. We've got to leave. Now!"

She practically pushed Gallagher and Stephanie out of Fernando's trailer.

"Enjoy your spaghetti," Gallagher said, as he was being shoved out the door.

"Um, thanks," Fernando said. "Glad I could help."

"We have to figure out what to do," Connie said as soon as they got into Gallagher's car.

"What is going on with you, Connie? What are you talking about?" Gallagher asked.

"Ronnie is the one with the gambling problem," Connie said. "Not Dom."

"I got that," Gallagher said. "But why did we just give Fernando the bum's rush?"

"Because Ronnie, Evan, and Kendra all lied about Dom's gambling problem," Connie said.

"Wait a minute," Stephanie said. "Are you thinking that all three of them killed Arnold together?"

"No," Connie said, with a firm shake of her head. "I think Kendra was telling the truth. Or at least she thought she was."

"Wait a minute," Gallagher said. "Do you think Ronnie lied to Evan about Dom's gambling problem, and Evan inadvertently spread the lie to Kendra?"

"But Ronnie can't be the killer. He has an alibi for what happened at my house today," Stephanie said.

"That's why Ronnie couldn't have done it alone. He had to have had help," Connie said.

"If not Kendra, then who helped him?" Stephanie asked.

"I'll explain when we get there. Whether my theory is correct or not, we need to get to Ronnie's and Dom's vacation rental right away. If Ronnie finds out that we talked to Judy, he might figure out that we know Dom is not the one with the gambling problem. Dom and Judy could be in danger."

Chapter 19

WHILE GALLAGHER DROVE to the vacation rental, Connie called Zach. But she got his voicemail. "Hey, Zach, I'm with Stephanie and Gallagher. I think I know who killed Arnold. Call me as soon as you can. We're afraid Dom and his wife might be in danger."

Within ten minutes, they were in front of the men's rental house.

"Should we try calling Zach again?" Stephanie asked as Gallagher parked on the street in front of their house.

"No. I told him it was important. Zach will call as soon as he sees the message."

"What are we going to do if Ronnie is in there?" Stephanie asked.

"We'll just say we need to speak with Dom and Judy alone. Once we get them out of the house, I'll explain my theory. Our first priority is to get them out of harm's way. Hopefully, Judy didn't tell Ronnie about our conversation with her earlier."

"With any luck, Ronnie will be at a casino somewhere, and Dom and Judy will be in there alone," Gallagher said.

They followed the walkway to the front door and rang the doorbell. When nobody answered, Stephanie suggested that they might be at the beach.

"Let's try the lanai before we walk all the way over to the beach," Connie said.

They walked around to the back of the house and peered over the low fence. To Connie's relief, Dom and Judy were seated at a table.

"Perfect," Gallagher said. "It looks like we got here in time."

Just then, Dom and Judy glanced in their direction. *Was that fear on their faces?*

Dom made a motion with his hand as if he were pushing them away.

"I think they're trying to tell us something," Stephanie said. "Why are they just sitting at the table directly in the sun with nothing to drink?"

Connie felt goose bumps forming on her arms. "Something's not right."

Dom and Judy immediately looked in the other direction, as if pretending not to have seen them, but it was too late. Stephanie gasped as someone grabbed her firmly from behind and held a knife in front of her neck.

It was Evan.

Gallagher's face turned as white as the sand on Sapphire Beach. He looked at Connie with pleading eyes as the two of them followed Evan toward the lanai, staying as close to Stephanie as her captor permitted.

Evan led them to the back of the house, where they had a full view of the lanai.

Connie gasped.

Ronnie was standing a few feet away, holding Judy and Dom at gunpoint.

"You don't look surprised to see me," Evan said to Connie. Then he smirked in Ronnie's direction. "You were right. They *were* on to us."

"Are you guys okay?" Connie asked Dom and Judy.

They both nodded in unison. But Connie wasn't reassured.

"Ronnie and Evan conspired to kill Arnold," Dom blurted out.

"Let me guess," Connie said. "Ronnie is the one with the gambling debt, but he couldn't kill Arnold alone, because his motive would be too obvious. So, Ronnie promised Evan a cut from his portion of the sale if he went along with his plan."

"Evan's relationship with Kendra worked to his advantage," Dom said. He looked angrily at Evan. "I'll bet you only got involved with her, because you knew she wanted to purchase the magazine, and you didn't want to lose your job if that happened."

Evan laughed. "She's going to promote me and give me a pay raise. Even without the cut from Ronnie, it still would have worked to my advantage for Kendra to be the new owner."

"Ronnie had to make sure Evan had an alibi so that the police would trust him," Connie said. "So, you made sure he was on the phone outside of *Gallagher's* at the time the food was delivered. Then

Evan started feeding everyone false information about Dom, so he would look like the guilty one."

"Evan played *everyone*," Judy said. "Kendra had no reason not to believe what Evan told her about Dom's supposed gambling problem."

"And we believed your lies because you had an alibi," Gallagher said.

Ronnie laughed. "I thought it was a nice touch that Evan left a note on your door saying he had some information about the case that he wanted to tell you," he said to Stephanie.

"Not to mention Evan saying in front of Dom that he was going to visit Fernando just before he disappeared," Connie added. "We thought Dom was the one trying to throw us off, but it was actually Evan."

Evan pushed Stephanie into a chair next to Judy and Dom and motioned for Connie and Gallagher to stand near them. "If any one of you tries to escape, you'll all be dead."

There was a stainless steel barbecue grill near where Connie and Gallagher were standing. Connie glanced over to see if there were any sharp utensils that she could take advantage of, but no such luck.

Then again, how useful would they really be when Ronnie had a gun and Evan had a knife?

"Where were you hiding?" Connie asked Evan, trying to stall.

"At a motel in Fort Myers," Evan said.

"So, it was Ronnie who left the salad in my house?" Stephanie asked.

They knew that it was Evan, since Zach had told Stephanie that both Dom and Ronnie had an alibi, but Connie guessed that Stephanie was trying to stall, as well.

"That was *my* handiwork," Evan boasted. "Ronnie made sure he had an alibi. I guess you could say I returned the favor of him giving me an alibi from last Friday night."

"Enough questions!" Ronnie yelled. "We need to think. Once your bodies are found, *I'm* the one who's going to look guilty, not Evan. We need an escape plan."

Connie glanced at Stephanie, who seemed to be trying to motion toward something with a discreet head gesture. She followed Stephanie's glance and noticed a tennis racket leaning against a potted palm tree.

Connie raised her eyebrows at Stephanie. *What good would a tennis racket do against a knife and a gun?*

The only advantage the group had was that they outnumbered Ronnie and Evan. But since Ronnie and Evan had the weapons, that seemed irrelevant.

Gallagher and Dom seemed to understand what Stephanie was getting at.

Don't try anything, guys, Connie thought. *It's* way *too risky.*

Before Connie could shake her head to discourage them, Gallagher leapt at Ronnie, who had the gun, and a shot fired. Saying a lightning-speed prayer that the bullet didn't hit anyone, Connie lept toward the tennis racket and took advantage of the moment of confusion to execute her newly acquired back hand swing. Evan fell to the ground, stunned, and Connie grabbed the knife from his hand.

Ronnie and Gallagher were still struggling, so at that point, Dom leapt from his chair and punched Ronnie in the stomach, giving Gallagher the upper hand. Literally.

Finally, Gallagher seized the gun and stepped back.

Dom pointed to the boat attached to their dock. "Honey, there's rope in the boat."

Judy sprinted on board and emerged a few seconds later with two long pieces of rope. She tossed one to Dom, who secured Ronnie, and Connie took the other and tied up Evan while Gallagher held him down.

"Thanks for helping me perfect my backhand," she said to Evan, as she tied his hands together.

Connie called 9-1-1, and a few minutes later, the sound of sirens approached in the distance.

"Zach never called you back," Stephanie said.

"That's because as soon as I got her message, I decided to come straight here."

At hearing Zach's voice, the tension of the previous ten minutes melted from Connie's shoulders.

While the police taped off the crime scene and made the necessary arrests, Connie stood next to Stephanie. "How are you doing? You were a hostage and you handled it like a champ."

"I'm okay," Stephanie said, smiling at Gallagher, who had refused to leave Ronnie's and Evan's side until they were in handcuffs. "I hope this means he can reopen the restaurant this weekend."

Then Stephanie turned toward Connie and winked. "But equally important, now that this case is solved, you can finally have that anniversary date with Zach."

Chapter 20

AFTER EVERYONE GAVE their statements at the Sapphire Beach Police Station, Dom and Judy walked to the parking lot with Connie, Gallagher, and Stephanie and thanked them for solving the case and coming to their aid.

"It would be an understatement to say that it's been a life-altering two weeks," Dom said. "Judy and I are flying home tomorrow evening, but it will take us a long time to move on from this horrific experience. I arrived in Sapphire Beach with Arnold, Ronnie, and Evan, and now I'm departing knowing that one is dead and the other two are in police custody."

"But there's one thing we are certain of," Judy said. "If Kendra is still interested in purchasing

Tennis Times, we're prepared to offer her a top-notch deal. We've arranged for a final meeting with her before our flight."

"I imagine she will be happy to hear that," Connie said. "We wish you all the best."

"Before we go, we have a gift for you," Dom said with a playful smile. "I'll be right back."

Dom returned with a tennis racket. "Since you mastered the backhand swing so quickly, we thought you might have a natural talent for the game," he said, handing her the racket.

They all shared a much-needed laugh as Connie gratefully accepted their gift.

After leaving the police station, the trio gathered at *Just Jewelry* to decompress and to fill in Abby on the details of their evening. Connie had called her on the way to the police station to give her a brief update and let her know she would be a lot later than anticipated, and Stephanie had called Grace, as well, who was also waiting for them at *Just Jewelry*.

When Connie arrived at her shop, she received a hero's welcome from Ginger, who enthusiastically greeted her when she came through the door.

Somehow, that little dog always knew when Connie needed some extra love.

It was nearly 9:00 by the time everyone arrived, so Connie flipped the "Open" sign on her front door to say "Closed," and everyone gathered at the large oak table. The three friends recounted everything that happened that evening, starting with their conversation with Fernando.

Grace made the Sign of the Cross, then scooted her chair closer to Stephanie and hugged her daughter tightly. "I can't believe my baby was a hostage. You kids should never have gone to that house alone."

"In hindsight, that may be true," Gallagher said. "But we were afraid that Dom and Judy would get hurt if we didn't get there right away. But I kept my promise. I didn't let anything happen to Stephanie."

"I can vouch for that," Connie said. "Gallagher was the first to stand up to Ronnie, even though he had a gun."

Grace shivered. "I'm glad I wasn't there."

"Now that the case is solved, let's focus on Gallagher's grand reopening," Connie said. "He was given permission to open anytime."

"I'm going to call all of my staff tonight to see if they can work tomorrow. I'm sure they would like the hours, and I could use the help getting the restaurant ready. I think we'll have a special theme for dinner to make it a celebration. I'm sure Fernando and I can come up with a few specials to add to the dinner menu tomorrow."

"As soon as you have the details, I'll make some fliers," Stephanie said. "How about if we all meet in the morning to hang them around town?"

"Perfect," Connie said. "Once you forward me the details, I'll create an event and share it on all my social media sites, both personal and business."

"Forward it to us so we can all share it, too," Abby said.

"Will do. Now that we have a plan in place, why don't we get some sleep so we can meet first thing in the morning to advertise the heck out of this event?" Grace said.

"Why don't we meet at 8:00 AM, before the store opens, so we can all hang fliers?"

And just like that, they had a plan.

They cheerfully left the store together. After Connie got home, she took Ginger for a long walk in hopes of tiring herself out since she was still wound up after a rollercoaster evening. Then she went upstairs to read herself to sleep.

As she was dozing off, Connie received a text message from Zach.

Don't forget, we have dinner reservations tomorrow night. This time, nothing is going to interfere with our plans.

Can't wait, Connie replied. *But can we meet at* Gallagher's *before dinner to have a drink? He's reopening for dinner tomorrow, and I'd like to stop by and offer my support.*

Our reservations are at 7. How about if I pick you up a little before 6 so we can drive to Gallagher's *together? Then we can go to the restaurant from there.*

Perfect, Connie replied. *See you then.*

The following morning, while Gallagher and his entire staff were cleaning the restaurant and prepping for dinner, Connie, Stephanie, Grace, Kelly, her son, Andy, Abby, and even Wes met in front of *Just Jewelry.* From there, they set off to hang fliers around town, leaving copies with the business owners they knew, and asking everyone they met to spread the word.

Since Gallagher was always generous with downtown workers when they ordered lunch from his restaurant, giving them extra fries or a complimentary smoothie, or offering free delivery when they couldn't break away, it was an easy sell. They were happy to return the favor by spreading the word about the special "Caribbean Night" that Gallagher and Fernando had cooked up to draw a crowd into his restaurant that evening.

The rest of the morning and afternoon were uneventful. Connie hadn't heard from Zach, but she didn't expect to, since he'd be busy tying up loose ends on the murder case.

Kelly and her husband, Stewart, had arranged for a babysitter for Andy that evening so they could come out to support Gallagher. Even though she didn't normally work on weekends, Kelly offered to cover the store for a while so Abby could stop in at *Gallagher's,* since Connie would be with Zach.

Everything was in motion. All that was left to do was await her date.

Abby arrived an hour early for her shift and insisted that Connie leave immediately to get ready for her date.

"It feels like we've done this before," Connie joked as she was leaving for the evening.

Abby laughed. "That's because we have. Two times!"

Connie took advantage of the extra time to get a French manicure and pedicure. She told herself it was a reward for solving the case, although she had to admit Elyse's comment about making sure her nails looked good just in case still echoed in her mind.

When she returned home, Connie brought Ginger for a long walk, giving her nails plenty of time to dry before hopping into the shower. Since this was their third attempt at this date, she already knew what she was going to wear. She had selected a blush floral dress with a light blush sweater in case the temperature dropped, and a matching blush and sapphire blue necklace, bracelet, and earring set she had purchased before it could make it to her Fair Trade section. She had loved it so much that she bought the dress to match the jewelry, rather than the other way around.

Zach arrived at 5:45 wearing a navy blazer and dress pants with a white shirt. He handed her a dozen red roses when he arrived, which she promptly put in a crystal vase and placed on her dining room table.

"We should get going so we have some time to spend at *Gallagher's* before our reservation," Zach said after Connie finished arranging the flowers.

It was a beautiful, warm evening, and the comforting smell of the salty air was working its magic after eight harrowing days.

When they arrived at *Gallagher's*, the restaurant was hopping. Elyse and Josh were about to order food at the bar, and Grace and Stephanie were seated next to them.

Fernando had outdone himself with the new Caribbean dishes and, according to Stephanie, was trying to convince Gallagher to make them a permanent addition. Since they didn't want to take up seats that food-ordering customers could occupy, Connie and Zach opted to stand near their friends with their glasses of Merlot.

Just as Connie and Zach were about to leave, Abby and Wes arrived. Abby was gushing as she introduced Wes to everyone and retold the story of how they met.

Gallagher popped over to the bar in between helping his staff deliver food to tables. He smiled from ear to ear as he looked out onto his dining room, which was bursting at the seams. "It looks like *Gallagher's Tropical Shack* is not merely going to survive," he said. "If tonight is any indication, we're going to thrive."

"We're thrilled for you," Elyse said. "We'll continue to talk up the restaurant."

"And the business owners we talked to today when we were dropping off fliers promised to continue to spread the word, as well," Connie added.

The conversation gradually moved to the case. Elyse was the only one who hadn't been closely following all the details, so they caught her up on what had happened the night before.

After they had caught Elyse up to speed, it suddenly occurred to Connie that they had been at *Gallagher's Tropical Shack* for quite a while. She had been so wrapped up in the moment, that she completely forgot to keep an eye on the time. In a panic, she glanced at her phone. It was 7:05.

"Oh, no!" she said to Zach. "We missed our reservation."

Zach, who was leaning against a bar stool and smiling at Connie, shook his head. "Don't worry about that. You looked radiant talking with your friends, so I decided we're meant to spend this evening right here, sharing it with the people who help make Sapphire Beach feel like home. I called the restaurant a few minutes ago to let them know we wouldn't be coming."

Zach whispered something to Gallagher, then took Connie's hand and led her to a table for two that a busser had just cleaned off. Zach stepped in front of the hostess, who was accompanying another couple to the table. "Excuse me," he said to her. "I need to borrow this table. We'll only be a few minutes."

The confused hostess looked at Gallagher, who winked and nodded his approval.

Connie and Zach sat at the small table beneath a blue and white surfboard hung on a driftwood accent wall, much like the wall in Connie's own shop. There was a picture window next to them, through which Connie could see the familiar street where her shop was located, the old weather-beaten pier, and crystal blue waters dancing in the distance.

"I tried my absolute best to do this at sunset at *White Sands Grill,* because I know it's one of your favorite places. But I just don't think it was meant to happen that way."

Zach glanced toward the bar, where so many of their friends watched them, then he fixed his blue eyes on Connie. "Our important dates have always been marked by the unexpected. It's one of the things I love about our relationship."

Connie thought back to their first date, when they went parasailing and Connie figured out where Natasha's body was located, and their second date eight months later, when they happened upon a missing person who was crucial to a murder investigation.

Zach stood up from his chair and knelt on one knee. He pulled a small velvet box from his pocket. "Connie Petretta, I love you and I can't imagine my life without you. Our relationship is a beautiful adventure that I never want to end. Will you give me the honor of walking through this life by your side? Will you marry me?"

As Connie watched Zach before her on one knee, she felt as if her heart would burst from the happiness she felt. There wasn't a doubt in her mind as to what her answer would be.

"Yes!" she said, placing her trembling hand in his.

He slipped the ring on her finger. They stood up and embraced until the cheerful sound of clapping pulled them from the moment. The next thing Connie heard was a loud squeal coming from the direction of the bar. "I knew it!"

It was Elyse.

Connie wiped tears of joy from her eyes. It looked like Elyse had been right this time.

"You're not disappointed that we didn't make it to your favorite restaurant?" Zach asked Connie as they walked arm in arm toward their friends, whose faces reflected the joy in Connie's heart.

"Are you kidding? After tonight, *Gallagher's Tropical Shack* is officially my new favorite restaurant."

After spending some time celebrating with their friends, they left to call their families to share with them the good news.

Before Connie even hung up with her family, her mother, Jo, and sister, Gianna, had already booked their next flight to southwest Florida.

They had a wedding to plan.

Next Book in this Series

Book 11: *Daffodils and Death*

Paperback bundles are available at Angela's store. Visit:
store.angelakryan.com/collections/paperback-bundles
to save with a bundle.

Individual books are available on Amazon.

OR

Free Prequel: *Vacations and Victims*.

Meet Concetta and Bethany in the
Sapphire Beach prequel.

Available in ebook or PDF format only at:

BookHip.com/MWHDFP

Stay in touch!

Join my Readers' Group for periodic updates, exclusive content, and to be notified of new releases. Enter your email address at: BookHip.com/MWHDFP

OR

Email:
angela@angelakryan.com

Facebook:
facebook.com/AngelaKRyanAuthor

Post Office:
Angela K. Ryan, John Paul Publishing, P.O. Box 283, Tewksbury, MA 01876

MEET THE AUTHOR

Angela K. Ryan is the author of the *Sapphire Beach Cozy Mystery Series* and the *Seaside Ice Cream Shop Mysteries*. She writes clean, feel-good cozies for readers who love humor, lots of twists and turns, and happy-dance endings.

When she is not writing, Angela enjoys the outdoors, especially kayaking, stand-up paddleboarding, snowshoeing, and skiing. She lives in Massachusetts and loves all four of the New England seasons, but she looks forward to regular escapes to the white, sandy beaches of southwest Florida, where her mother resides.

It is fitting that Angela's two series take place in fictitious seaside towns in Massachusetts and Florida. These small towns would be idyllic if it weren't for all the bodies that keep turning up!

Angela dreams of one day owning a Cavalier King Charles Spaniel like the sweet pup in her *Sapphire Beach Series*, but she isn't home enough to take care of one. So, for now, lives vicariously through one of her main characters, Connie.

Made in the USA
Columbia, SC
25 May 2024

36181038R00145